Between Love and Death

Between Love and Death is a work of fiction. Names, characters, places, and incidents are the product of the author's imagination or are used fictitiously. Any resemblance to actual events, locales, or persons, living or dead, is coincidental.

Copyright © 2024 Chris Bedell

Between the Lines Publishing and its imprints supports the right to free expression and the value of copyright. The scanning, uploading, and distribution of this book without permission is a theft of the author's intellectual property. If you would like permission to use material from the book (other than for review purposes), please contact info@btwnthelines.com.

Willow River Press
Between the Lines Publishing
1769 Lexington Ave N, Ste 286
Roseville, MN 55113
btwnthelines.com

First Published: January 2025

ISBN Paperback: 978-1-965059-16-6
ISBN eBook: 978-1-965059-17-3

Willow River Press is an imprint of Between the Lines Publishing.
The Willow River Press name and logo are trademarks of Between the Lines Publishing.

The publisher is not responsible for websites (or their content) that are not owned by the publisher.

Between Love and Death

Chris Bedell

BEFORE

THURSDAY, JUNE 6

Lies always unravel.

Like the wife who discovered her husband was having an affair with the nanny. Or the teenager who forged their parent's signature. Or the bar that disguised low quality liquor by putting booze in top shelf bottles. Or even my lie about Mallory killing Tommy.

Archie smiled at me while we sat at a table in front of Starbucks, sipping our iced caramel macchiatos. However, my pulse hammered in my ears. Two months had passed since I visited Mallory at the sanitarium, yet my luck could change. Saying one wrong thing could make my situation implode.

Archie squeezed my hand. "Something wrong, babe? Did the barista not use enough caramel?"

I averted my gaze. "My drink is fine."

"Then what is it?"

I scratched the side of my head. "It's nothing."

He bit his lip. "Sorry. Should be more sensitive."

"What are you talking about?"

Archie sighed. "You're probably upset about your mother, right?"

1

Between Love and Death

The lump lingered in my throat. "Yeah."

He patted my hand. "I'm not gonna force you to discuss anything you don't want to. But I'm always here for you if you need to vent."

"Thanks." I sipped my beverage, but the mixture of the sweet caramel and bitter espresso flavors escaped me. Discussing how Mom was dying of stage four cancer wasn't something that rolled off my tongue, especially when I already lost my father. So, I'd soon have to live with being an orphan—whether I wanted to or not.

"Are you angry she isn't pursuing treatment?" he asked.

"What do you think?" I snapped.

Archie remained silent. Yikes. I should've been more careful. Being overwhelmed with emotions was one thing, but I couldn't alienate Archie. Not after I risked everything to be with him. So, I'd have to be more careful with Archie in the future. Having a thought didn't mean I actually had to verbalize it.

"Sorry. Shouldn't have been curt," I continued.

He massaged my back. "Don't worry about it. I'd be a mess if my mother declined chemo."

I sobbed. "This was supposed to be the best summer of our lives..."

"Yeah. I wasn't as happy when I finished my last final yesterday as I thought I'd be."

"Don't mean to be a downer."

"Stop! If we're gonna make this relationship work, then we've gotta be honest with each other."

"I know, I know."

Archie's lips quivered. "Mind if I say something?"

"Go ahead."

"Make the most of the time you have with your mother. Living with regret is the worst."

"True."

"Don't leave anything unsaid. Once she's gone, that's it," Archie said.

2

"I'm aware of that."

Archie coughed into his right arm. "Why don't we change the subject?"

"Sure. That'd be nice." I finished the rest of my beverage, then tossed it into an adjacent garbage.

"Your behavior about the Mallory situation has been impressive."

I blinked. "Huh?"

"I'm not kidding."

Someone must've slipped LSD into my drink. Archie couldn't have mentioned Mallory. We were free of that scheming interloper and that was the way our relationship needed to stay. Nothing good would come from discussing Mallory. She needed to rot in the sanitarium for the rest of her life. It was what she deserved.

And no, I wasn't being harsh. Mallory was a psychotic nutcase. Being upset about me rejecting her was one thing, but she shouldn't have gone *Single White Female* by taking Archie from me. She started this sick game between us. So, being in a mental institution was her fault. It wasn't like I got pleasure in ruining Mallory's life—I hadn't physically harmed her. I just wanted her gone.

"Let's not talk about that lunatic," I said.

Archie snickered. "I can't believe you let go of all your anger about Mallory. Don't think I'd be able to do that."

"Whatever," I whispered.

He elbowed me. "I'm not kidding, Chad. You have every reason to hate her, yet you aren't dwelling on the past."

"I got the closure I needed when I visited her that day in April."

Someone cackled. "I'm not so sure about that."

Footsteps echoed against the sidewalk, growing louder with each subsequent second. I lifted my gaze off the table. Mallory stood in front of us.

"The fuck are you doing here?" I stammered.

Mallory giggled. "Nice to see you, too, Chad."

Between Love and Death

Archie grabbed his iPhone from his pocket. "I'm calling the police. Time to send you back to the looney bin."

"I wouldn't do that if I were you," she said.

I choked. "No?"

Mallory clapped her hands. "I've been released from the mental hospital."

"You've gotta be fucking kidding me," I said.

"You might wanna stop cursing, sweetheart." Mallory flipped her hair over her shoulders. "That kind of language isn't gonna make for a prestigious college essay."

I almost spat in her face. "Fuck you, Mallory!"

Mallory leaned closer to me. "No thanks."

Archie grabbed me right when I was about to stand. Then he cocked his head. "You haven't told us how you're out."

"That part is simple," Mallory said.

"We don't have time for your games," I said.

Mallory snorted. "I won my appeal."

Archie glared at Mallory. "You can't appeal a guilty plea."

"Normally, you'd be correct," Mallory said.

I hissed at Mallory. "Get to the point. You've already ruined enough of our afternoon."

"Kelly hired me a new lawyer and we argued ineffective counsel," Mallory said.

"Come again?" I asked.

"The insanity defense wasn't my choice." Mallory put her hands on her hips while remaining silent for a beat, almost as if she wanted to practice her dramatic pauses for when she'll be cast in a movie. "My previous lawyer pressured me into the deal."

"You bitch," I said.

Mallory eyed me. "Do yourself a favor and invent a more original insult. Even you aren't that dumb."

"So, what?" Archie demanded. "You're free?"

4

Chris Bedell

"Yup," Mallory said.

I furrowed my brow. "When did you get released?"

"Less than an hour ago," Mallory revealed.

"How come this wasn't on the news?" I asked.

"I'm a minor, which means my privacy is protected," Mallory said.

Shit. Mallory might've been devious, but I couldn't argue with what she said. Her responses made sense. Her birthday wasn't till September.

"And Kelly went along with this?" I asked. "What about the fighting over your parents' money?"

"Sometimes people don't have a choice," Mallory said.

"The fuck is that supposed to mean?" I asked.

"That's for me to know and you to find out," Mallory replied.

Archie's Adam's apple throbbed. "What? You gonna kill us?"

Shit. Archie spent too much time with me. His comment was something I would've said. Death was the only way my toxic feud with Mallory would end. So, I wouldn't be surprised if one of us died by the end of senior year. Stranger things happened all the time. The world wasn't big enough for the two of us to coexist. Not after everything that transpired between us.

Mallory's hands fell to her sides. "One more thing."

"What?" I asked, raising my voice.

"I'm sorry about your mother's ovarian cancer, Chad," Mallory said. "That can't be easy. So, please let me know if I can do anything for you."

"Like you care," I said.

"I'm serious." Mallory exhaled. "No matter how awful things are between us, I wouldn't wish bad on your mother. Nobody deserves to die of cancer. Your mother isn't even forty-five years old."

I pounded my fist against the table, then Archie's grip on my shirt tightened. "I don't wanna discuss my mother!" I exclaimed.

"Sure." Mallory's jaw trembled. "But it's great seeing you and Archie doing well. Gives me hope that my love life might improve one day."

"Go!" I screamed.

Between Love and Death

Mallory winked at me. "See you around, Chad."

Mallory strutted down the block without another word. She was soon out of sight, but my heart pounded faster. I couldn't fucking believe it. Mom's terminal diagnosis wasn't enough. Nope. The universe had to fuck with me even more.

"I'm sorry," Archie said.

"You didn't do anything."

"True." Archie sucked on his straw, sipping the rest of his caramel macchiato. "But I'm not an idiot. She taunted you."

For a fleeting moment, my pulse lowered. Good to know Archie wasn't fooled by Mallory's act. I didn't know what I'd do if Archie suggested giving Mallory a second chance. Because I wouldn't have been surprised if that happened. That would've been the type of thing the universe would've loved doing to me.

"There's one thing, though," he said.

"I'm listening."

"I'm not gonna tell you how to feel about Mallory—she's done you wrong numerous times," Archie said. "But you need to beat her at her own game."

"Okay?"

Archie fanned himself with his tee-shirt while sweat clung to his face. "Letting Mallory know you're on to her gives her what she wants."

"What are you getting at?" I asked.

"Keep your friends close and your enemies closer," Archie said. "Or at the very least, don't accost Mallory in public. Then, you'll seem like the crazy one."

My mind drifted back to my earlier thought about how my turbulent dynamic with Mallory wouldn't end till one of us was dead. Yeah. No doubt existed in my mind about how that statement was true. Mallory was a cancer that needed to be eradicated from my life. Only question was how soon I'd be rid of her. This was war. Game on.

AFTER

FRIDAY, DECEMBER 6

"I can't wait to end this once and for all," I said.

Gemma barreled down a new stretch of highway while my head remained pressed against the window. My throat tightened while everything that had happened over the last six months raced through my mind. But only one person could be blamed for everything bad that happened to me. Mallory. Destroying my relationship with Archie, and alienating me from Rebecca and Dan, wasn't enough for that psychotic maniac. Mallory also framed me for her older sister's, Kelly's, murder.

I scoffed. Hard to believe Kelly was dead. Seemed like yesterday that she killed Tommy while I secretly watched.

Gemma cocked her head. "I don't blame you. What happened to you was an abomination, Chad."

"Thanks for stating the obvious." I exhaled a long breath. Shit. I was gonna have to get better at thinking before speaking. Pushing Gemma away would be the dumbest thing I could do. Even damaged outcasts needed sidekicks. If it wasn't for her, then this whole evening wouldn't be possible.

"Sorry," I said.

7

Between Love and Death

"Don't worry about it." She stopped at a red light. "Can't imagine what your life must've been like behind bars."

"I really am thankful you helped me."

"I know, I know."

My jaw twitched. "Killing Mallory isn't bad, is it?"

She giggled. "How many times are we gonna have this conversation? Mallory needs to be punished for what she did to you. Because she can't just get away with everything she did."

"I owe you an apology," I said.

"For what?"

I chewed on the inside of my lip. "I wasn't honest with you about my relationship with Tommy. We had sex more than once."

Yeah. I was serious about what I just told Gemma. Concealing how Kelly was Tommy's real killer and not Mallory wasn't the only secret I initially hid. Tommy and I hooked up almost ten more times before he cut me out of his life. Almost as if our encounters were a drug that Tommy couldn't refuse.

She made a clicking sound with her tongue. "I know."

"Huh?" I asked.

"No offense, but it's obvious that you and Tommy weren't a one-night stand." Gemma resumed driving once the light changed to green. After she honked at the driver in front of us, that was.

"Thanks for not being angry."

"No worries."

I heaved a sigh. "I still regret what happened to Tommy. He didn't deserve to die. Just wanted you to know that."

"Do you mind if we change the subject?" she asked.

"Sure."

"You're the brave one," Gemma said. "Don't know how I'd continue with my life if I were you."

I tugged at the sides of my leather jacket. "What are you getting at?"

"I'm referring to your mother."

8

My attention returned to the window. "Let's not talk about her."

"Losing a mother so early in life is a travesty."

"No point dwelling on it. Nothing is gonna bring her back."

She laughed louder this time. "You don't have to put on a façade for me. Vent whenever you want."

Gemma deserved kudos for her bluntness. I wouldn't have done the same if I were her. There was no polite way to discuss the loss of a friend's parent; the subject was unpleasant, and couldn't be spun no matter how much someone tried .

"I'll keep that in mind," I said.

Gemma took her eyes off the road for a beat and gazed at me. "I'm sure your mother loved you very much."

I opened my mouth, yet words escaped me. I couldn't swallow the lump in my throat—not this time. Gemma was right about her comment. Someone as young as I shouldn't have to grapple with their mother dying of cancer. But I couldn't escape the truth about Mom. She was dead. And there wasn't anything I could do about said fact. It wasn't like time travel existed. Nope. This was real life—not a science fiction movie.

So, yeah. Whether I accepted the truth or not, my life was a walking nightmare—I couldn't wake up from this unfortunate reality. And I'd do what I always did. Learn to live with the pain.

"At least things improved for you," I said.

"Inheriting fifty million dollars and becoming emancipated will do that."

"Thanks for paying the bills for my house while I was away," I said.

"Wasn't about to let the bank repossess your home."

"Do you think I'll ever find peace?" I asked.

Gemma snorted. "Once Mallory is dead."

Gemma pulled into Mallory's driveway a few minutes later while the moonlight glinted against the ground. She turned the car off, removed the keys from the ignition, then shoved them into her jacket pocket. After that, Gemma resumed eye contact. "Ready?" she asked.

I nodded. "Yes."

"Good." Gemma exited the car, then I trailed behind her while wind swooshed through the air and tree branches creaked.

My teeth chattered while we approached the front door. Yeah. Definitely wasn't June anymore. The chill in the air was so distinct that it might as well already have been winter even though it was technically fall for a couple of more weeks.

Gemma rang the doorbell.

The door opened, revealing Archie.

Archie's jaw lowered. "What are you two doing here?"

Interesting. Good to know that was how Archie greeted me. Apparently, hoping for a grin or a "nice to see you" was too much. I shouldn't have been surprised, though. Dynamics changed all the time. So, it wasn't like Archie and I would slip into a familiar pattern the moment he saw me. Only a miracle worker could accomplish that.

"Can we come in?" I asked.

Archie crossed his arms, wrinkling his ugly Christmas sweater. "Not sure that's a good idea. Besides, shouldn't you be in jail?"

I snickered. "I'll fill you on the details if you let me inside."

"Don't think so," Archie said.

"Don't be a buzzkill," Gemma said.

"Who's at the door?" called out someone.

Footsteps echoed, growing more distinct with each passing moment. Mallory arrived and now stood by Archie.

Mallory gritted her teeth. "What are you doing here?"

"It's quite the story," I said.

"Enough stalling, we're coming in whether you like it or not." Gemma grabbed my hand and dragged me into the house.

Mallory locked the door behind us, and Gemma and I stopped after spotting Dan and Rebecca. They sat on the living room couch, enjoying eggnog and appetizers. And I would've chuckled if I didn't have more important things to focus on. Nothing like making a dramatic entrance by crashing a party.

Dan's eyes widened. "Chad?"

"What the fuck are you doing here?" Rebecca asked.

"Getting the revenge I deserve." I whipped out a gun from my leather jacket's inside pocket. I pointed the weapon at Mallory, fingers gripping the trigger tighter than a python suffocating its prey. In fact, the gun would've fired if I held it any tighter.

Archie gave me a dirty look. "You can't bring a gun to a party, man."

I stepped closer to Mallory, hands still on the gun. "Give me one reason why I shouldn't fucking kill you."

Rebecca stood. "If you're upset about something, then we can discuss it. There's no reason to kill Mallory."

Gemma rolled her eyes. "Little late for that."

Mallory whimpered. "Tell us why you're here."

"Don't play innocent with me!" I exclaimed.

"I have no idea what you're getting at," Mallory said.

"You're too young for Dementia, Mallory," Gemma touted.

Bless Gemma. I couldn't have been more thankful to have Gemma as my best friend if I tried. Matching Mallory jab for jab was something my best friend needed to do. Mallory was a terrible person and needed to be insulted as much as possible. It was what she deserved after the chain of events she started. Hard to believe one person could cause so much destruction, yet she had.

Mallory pushed a lock of hair behind her ear. "Cute."

My spine tingled while my pulse soared. I couldn't believe this. After months of losing, I was in control. And that feeling was fucking great. Mallory deserved to have the tables turned on her because she couldn't get away with what she did to me. Not if there was any justice in the world.

Between Love and Death

Archie shot me a pleading look. "Please tell us why you're angry. Then, maybe we can help you."

"Mallory admitted everything to me," I said.

"What do you mean?" Dan asked.

"Mallory framed me for Kelly's murder," I said, my heart thumping faster and louder. Dragging Mallory was beyond great. Crucifying Mallory needed to happen—whether she wanted it to or not. Mallory turned Archie, Dan, and Rebecca against me, and I was gonna do the same to her. Only fair.

"It's true," Mallory said. "I confessed to framing Chad for my sister's murder when I visited him in jail."

Archie gasped. "Are you serious?"

"Yeah, Chad is right." Mallory paused for a beat. "But I don't see what the big deal is. You only spent a few months behind bars. Besides, you haven't told us how you're free."

"I bribed the District Attorney to drop the charges, and the judge went along with it," Gemma said. "One less case to clog up the court docket."

I hissed. "Gemma!"

"Relax," Gemma said. "Not like they can prove what we did."

Mallory nodded. "You're right. I can't prove what you did. But you're still making a big deal out of nothing, Chad. You're getting a second chance, so don't mess up your life this time. Your mother wouldn't approve."

I lunged closer to Mallory—so close that my breath might've prickled her skin. "Don't mention my mother, you filthy bitch! If you hadn't framed me for Kelly's murder, then I wouldn't have been denied bail, and then I would've been able to attend my mother's funeral. Imagine that. Me not being able to say goodbye to my mom."

Archie shifted his attention to Mallory. "He has a point. How could you do that to Chad? You knew his mother was dying of cancer."

12

Mallory made a fist. "Have you forgotten how Chad knew Kelly killed Tommy, yet framed me for it?"

"Nothing happened to you at the sanitarium," I quipped. "But the same can't be said for me."

Rebecca adjusted her posture on the couch. "I'm afraid to ask…"

"I was burned with a cigarette lighter, in addition to how I was nearly beaten to death," I said. "So spare me the bullshit about how prison wasn't a big deal."

Archie clapped his hand over his mouth.

"But if you don't believe me, then I'd be happy to remove my jacket and shirt and show you my scar from where I was burned with the cigarette lighter," I continued.

Dan and Rebecca exchanged a horrified look.

"That won't be necessary," Archie said.

Mallory smiled. "Maybe you shouldn't have lied."

"Have you forgotten this whole thing started because you took Archie from me after being pissed that I didn't reciprocate your crush?" I asked.

Yeah. I'd never forget the first day of junior year. Not even if I got a lobotomy. It was challenging to admit that one person could have such a large impact on my life; however, it was even more difficult to accept that my life changed in such a short amount of time. The image of me catching Mallory lurking nearby after I flirted with Archie the first day of junior year would never disappear from my mind no matter how much I tried forgetting the incident. Mallory's stalking behavior should've been my first clue about how demented she was. Maybe then I'd be still be with Archie and I wouldn't have spent time in jail while awaiting trial.

Exploiting weaknesses was what predators like Mallory did, though. With her, that meant Mallory counted on the small part of me who believed our friendship was salvageable. The part of me who was nostalgic and hoped the good times between us weren't over.

Between Love and Death

But no. Mallory made it her mission to ruin my life after I revealed I didn't feel the same way about her.

"Okay. I've made a few mistakes," Mallory said.

"Putting someone in a position where they almost get beaten to death isn't a mistake." I smacked Mallory's face with the gun in one swift motion. Then, Mallory stepped backward, almost losing her balance.

"Tell me something," I said. "Can you bring back my mother? What about making it so my beating never happened?"

"I'm so sorry, Chad," Mallory said.

"Empty words," Gemma piped in.

Mallory grunted. "Shut the fuck up, Gemma!"

"I'm not afraid of you," Gemma said.

Mallory shook her head. "You should be."

Archie turned back to me. "So, what? You're gonna kill Mallory?"

Perhaps Archie wasn't as clueless as I suspected. Good of him to realize what was about to happen. Mallory deserved to die, and nothing anybody said would change my mind. It couldn't. Death was the ultimate revenge for what Mallory did to me.

"Yes," I said.

"You'd throw your life away so you can murder Mallory?" Archie put his hands in his pockets.

"Yup," I said, nodding.

Archie's face drooped. "You deserve another chance at life."

"Not like you'll take me back," I said.

"I'm sorry for how things turned out between us," Archie said.

I grunted. "Have you been paying attention to anything I've said? It's too late for apologies."

"Chad isn't going to jail," Gemma said. "I'll help him. That's one of the perks of being a millionaire."

"You're new money, not old money," Mallory said.

Please. Mallory should've considered her comment before speaking. It didn't matter how Gemma obtained her money. The point was,

14

Chris Bedell

Gemma was rich. So, Gemma could do whatever the fuck she wanted. And Mallory must've been jealous. I would've been jealous of Gemma if I were Mallory. Hard not to be. Gemma was everything Mallory wasn't. Empathetic. Successful. Resourceful.

"Doesn't matter. Besides, Chad would be doing a public service by killing you," Gemma said. "Chad didn't deserve to be nearly beaten to death."

"There's more," I blurted.

"Excuse me?" Archie asked.

"Mallory didn't kill Tommy, but she is guilty of other crimes," I said, not changing my mind about pointing the gun at Mallory.

"Yeah, we know how Mallory is guilty of obstruction of justice and other possible things by framing you for Kelly's murder," Archie said.

"I'm not talking about that," I said.

"Then what?" Archie demanded.

I drew in a deep breath. No undoing my bombshell about Parker and Jordon once I dropped it. So, I was gonna have to make sure I could live with revealing this information. Outing Mallory's other secret meant losing my additional leverage over Mallory.

I pressed the gun against Mallory's chin and her lips quivered. "Wanna tell them? Or should I?"

Rebecca twirled a strand of hair around her finger. "Don't think I can take any more of this conversation."

I smirked. "You're gonna wanna hear this next bit. Promise."

Sweat dripped down Mallory's face. "Chad, please!"

"It's also too late for groveling," I said.

"Fine!" Mallory shouted. "I'll admit it. I killed Parker and Jordon because they cheated on their girlfriends. And I admitted this to Chad when he visited me at the sanitarium last April. Even Kelly was suspicious—she kept the newspaper articles about Parker's and Jordon's deaths in her safe."

15

Rebeca stood, then arched an eyebrow. "If Chad didn't kill Kelly, then does that mean you did?"

Rebecca's interruption might've irked me. Her question only delayed the inevitable—killing Mallory. But she raised a valid point. There were still a lot of things about Kelly's death that didn't make sense. Like why her dead body never appeared. The TV binge watcher in me couldn't forget that mantra. No dead body usually meant the person was still alive the majority of the time.

"That's not important," Mallory said.

"I'm done," I said, gun still facing Mallory. "Any last words before I pull the trigger?"

"Yes, but not here," Mallory said.

"Come again?" I asked.

Mallory rubbed her eye. "Let's talk in private."

"Don't think so," I said.

"It's not a trap," Mallory said. "Having a gun means you've got the advantage."

Shit. When Mallory was right, she was right. Even if I would've rather fallen into a volcano than compliment Mallory.

"Fine. You have two minutes," I said.

SATURDAY, DECEMBER 7

It was a little after midnight.

So, only a couple of hours went by since I crashed Mallory's party.

The elevator chimed, then Gemma and I exited it before shuffling toward the hospital's waiting room.

Archie, Dan, and Rebecca were seated in chairs. Dan and Rebecca remained glued to their iPhones, but Archie just tapped his feet against the tile floor.

Archie stood the second he met my gaze. "What are you doing here?"

"I came to check on Mallory," I said.

Chris Bedell

Archie pulled me to the side. "You shouldn't be here."

"If I'm being honest, then I've gotta admit that I was a bit disappointed by how you greeted me at the party," I said.

"This is no time for games," Archie said.

I folded my arms. "Answer my question."

"Mallory is still in surgery," Archie responded.

"Cool."

Archie looped his arms around my neck. "You've gotta get out of here. What if the police stop by? Hospitals have to report gunshot wounds."

"Careful. Might think you care."

"I'm serious."

"Have the police dropped by?" I asked.

"Not yet," Archie said. "But they're going to ask us where we all were. Especially since Mallory's house was set up for a party."

Color me impressed. Archie was considering every element of the situation. So maybe, just maybe, if I needed someone to help me cover up a crime, then Archie was my guy. I could do worse, after all.

I made a pig-like snort. "Feeling guilty about how you, Rebecca, and Dan left Mallory alone waiting for the ambulance?"

"You did the same."

I put my hands on my hips. "I know. But at least I can own my messy behavior. That's more than can be said about you, Rebecca, and Dan."

"Leave!" Archie exclaimed.

"It wasn't supposed to be like this," I said.

Archie scowled. "You showed up to a party with a gun! What did you expect?"

"Truthfully, Mallory seemed like she had a trick up her sleeve." I cracked my knuckles. "Anyway, we can always invent some cover story. Like what if you, Dan, and Rebecca bailed on Mallory's party because she was having a personal crisis?"

17

Between Love and Death

Archie grimaced. "What if someone saw us arriving or leaving Mallory's house?"

Being careful and calculating was one thing. But Archie now bordered on being a buzzkill. Mallory's neighbors must've had better things to do than watch who was arriving and leaving her house.

"I'm sure you're fine," I said.

His shoulders shook. "And you left the gun by Mallory's side?"

Enough with the questions. I might not have been perfect, but I wasn't an idiot. I was capable of deep thinking, too. It wasn't like I wanted to return to jail. And I wasn't even referring to the possibility of getting almost beaten to death again.

"The police need to think it was an accident. Maybe she was drunk, got a little depressed, and shot herself," I said. "Besides, my prints were wiped off the gun in addition to how the serial number was removed from the gun."

"You've got everything figured out, don't you?" Archie asked.

I let out a breath. "I'm doing what I have to do to survive. In case you didn't realize, I haven't had a cushy life the last few months like the rest of you."

Yeah. I'd never stop throwing the last few months in Archie's face. Maybe then he'd have a faint clue about what my life was like. While he wondered about which colleges to apply to, I wondered if I was gonna get beaten to death again.

Archie looked me over. "I've only got one question for you."

Interesting. If I didn't know better, then I would've thought Archie wanted to prolong the conversation. Almost as if my earlier comment about how he still might've cared was true. Lingering feelings might've been a good thing, though. That could be something I could exploit if necessary. No telling what the future would hold.

I winked. "And what's that?"

"Are you sleeping with Gemma?" Archie asked.

BEFORE

FRIDAY, JUNE 14

Mom and I sat on stools in front of the kitchen counter. A whole week had passed since Mallory was released, yet my pulse hadn't stopped pounding in my ears. I was gonna have to take control of the Mallory situation. I just didn't know what that would entail.

Mom raised an eyebrow at me. "Something wrong, honey?"

I averted my gaze, focusing on the screeching crow outside the kitchen window. I didn't know whether I should be honest with Mom or not about Mallory's release from the sanitarium. On the one hand, I didn't wanna burden Mom. On the other hand, Mom might feel good having a distraction.

She squeezed my hand. "You don't have to be secretive with me. Let me be your mother for as long as I can."

"Mallory's been released," I blurted.

"I know."

I fidgeted on the stool, resuming eye contact with Mom. "How?"

"I saw her in town a couple of days ago."

Way to bury the lede. Apparently, Mom was better at keeping secrets than I realized. And said fact was great. It wasn't as if life wasn't

19

complicated enough with Mallory. So, yeah, I couldn't help wondering what else Mom kept from me.

"And you didn't say anything?" I asked, raising my voice.

Mom sipped her coffee. "I didn't know if it was still a touchy subject. Clearly, I was right to go with my gut."

"Fair enough."

"I know it's none of my business, but you can vent to me if you want. Promise not to get mad or think you're neurotic."

I bit my lip. For a split second, I wanted to tell Mom the truth about everything. Like how I ensured Mallory would get in trouble for Tommy's murder despite how I knew Mallory didn't kill him.

She heaved a sigh. "You're my son, and nothing will stop me from loving you."

Interesting. It was as if Mom read my mind. Mom might not have blatantly said it, but it was as if she knew I was hiding something.

"There's no coming back from this one," I said.

Her gaze narrowed. "It can't be that bad."

"I'll tell you everything if you promise to keep this between us."

Yeah. I was gonna confide in Mom about everything because I didn't have a choice. I needed to unload this burden onto someone. Mom couldn't change what already happened, but she might have good advice. It wasn't like my life could get any worse. Mom wouldn't blab to Archie about what I did. She wasn't that type of person. I hoped not, at least.

Mom didn't even blink. "Absolutely."

"Mallory didn't kill Tommy. Kelly did." I paused for a beat. "But I worked to frame Mallory for the murder. I even visited Mallory at the sanitarium and confessed everything just so I could get the last word."

Mom gaped. "You did what?"

"I'm not proud of it, but I couldn't help myself." I scratched an itch on the back of my neck. "Mallory was never gonna leave my relationship with Archie alone."

Chris Bedell

"You did this because of a boy?" Mom chugged the rest of her coffee, then put it in the sink.

No offense to Mom, but she needed to lose the contempt in her voice. I was only a teenager, so I was allowed to make mistakes. It wasn't like Archie encouraged me to become a serial killer. I just wanted Mallory out of my life. I saw her for what she was, and I wouldn't let myself get sucked in. I couldn't. Not after everything Mallory did.

My eyebrows knitted together. "Weren't you not supposed to judge me?"

"You're right, I'm sorry." Mom looped her arms around my neck, then stared me down. "Thanks for telling me the truth. That couldn't have been easy for you."

"There's more," I said.

"Do I even wanna know?"

"Mallory didn't murder Tommy, but she did kill Parker and Jordon. I don't know if you remember their deaths..."

"How could you possibly know that?" Mom demanded.

"Because Mallory confessed to me."

"And let me guess. Archie has no idea about what you did?"

"Archie knows I framed Mallory, but he's not mad. He still thinks Mallory is responsible for Tommy's death."

"Do you think Mallory is gonna expose you?" Mom asked.

I shrugged. "Don't know. I mean, I'm sure Mallory would relish in outing my secret. Although I'm not sure about whether she'd wanna give up her leverage over me so quickly."

"Do you wanna make your relationship with Archie work?" Mom asked.

I nodded.

"Then you need to tell Archie the truth yourself," Mom continued. "Not because you did a bad thing and deserve to be punished or it's never okay to lie. But because it'll be better if Archie hears this from you rather than Mallory."

Between Love and Death

When Mom was right, she was right. But there was a big difference between agreeing with an idea and implementing it. If I told Archie what I did, then he might breakup with me. And I couldn't have that. Not after I worked so hard to be Archie's boyfriend. However, I also hated Mallory having leverage over me.

"Thanks for the advice, Mom."

She giggled. "You don't have to thank me for anything."

"Most people would think I'm a terrible person if they discovered what I did."

"I'm not most people." Mom laughed louder this time. "Although the sex with Archie better be worth all this scheming."

"Mom!" I exclaimed.

"I'm sorry. I can't help it."

An awkward silence ensued for a moment. I should've chastised Mom more about her racy comment. But I didn't. An obscene joke was what the conversation needed to lighten the mood. And Mom was also once again right. Good sex was the least that should've happened. I couldn't imagine going to such extreme lengths to save a relationship over some boring guy.

"There's something else we need to discuss," Mom said.

"And what's that?"

"You're disappointed I'm not pursuing chemo. Don't deny it."

I stood before pushing my stool in. "Don't wanna discuss that."

"I'm an adult, so let me have it."

Mom had to have been joking. There was no way we'd have this conversation. It was Mom's body, and she had a right not to pump toxins into it if that was what she wanted. I also didn't wanna spend what little time she had left fighting. Bickering with Mom would only leave me with regret. And that was the last thing I needed after everything that happened to me.

I grunted. "It is what it is."

"I'm not angry if you hoped for a different outcome."

22

Chris Bedell

"I have enough problems as it is."

Mom ran her fingers through her hair. "At least I'm not gonna go bald."

The old me might've scoffed at Mom's comment—some jokes were too morbid even for me. Yet I wouldn't begrudge Mom her remark. Not when I had bigger issues to focus on. Like whether or not I'd tell Archie the truth about what I did to Mallory. I could only delay the issue for so long because Mallory would be been planning something big. And the only question was how much damage she'd do to my life.

Mom pursed her lips. "All joking aside, I hope you solve your problem with Mallory."

I forced a small smile. "Thanks."

"I'm serious."

"There's a simple solution."

"And what's that?" Mom asked.

"I could kill her."

Mom scowled. "You've got to be kidding?"

"Could make it look like an accident. Maybe she got a little drunk and lost her temper, so I did what was necessary to defend myself."

Mom shook her head.

"I'm kidding," I continued.

"Good."

I coughed, clearing the uneasiness from my throat. "There's a less violent option. I could always drug Mallory with sedatives, so she'd blackout and lose time. You know. Make people think she was mentally ill."

"You'd really do that?" Mom asked.

"Mallory's the one who started this bullshit."

Mom placed her hands on my hands. "Promise me you won't kill Mallory?"

My stomach knotted. I was only human, so that meant contemplating dark emotions even if I'd never act on them. But no. I wouldn't kill

Mallory. At least not in cold blood. I couldn't. I wasn't a monster. I just wanted her out of my life. However, the continued burning sensation pulsing through my stomach wasn't because I ate spoiled or spicy food. I was still privy to how my feud with Mallory wouldn't end till one of us was dead no matter how pure my intentions were. I just didn't see how the situation could have a positive outcome.

SUNDAY, JUNE 16

Rebecca, Dan, and I shuffled down the block while sunlight beamed against the ground. We were gonna see a movie and I couldn't be happier. I was finally doing something a "normal" person did.

My throat constricted before we walked down a new street. I still hadn't decided whether or not I'd tell Archie the truth.

Rebecca eyed me. "Something wrong, Chad?"

I shook my head. "I'm fine."

"You must be a little annoyed Archie couldn't join us for a double date," Dan said.

I exhaled a breath. "Not the end of the world that Archie has plans with his parents and sister."

Rebecca's hair bobbed in the wind. "I admire your attitude. Although there's something else we should discuss."

"And what's that?" I asked.

"We know Mallory is no longer at the mental hospital," Dan said.

I rolled my eyes. "Okay..."

"Why did you not say anything sooner?" Rebecca asked.

No offense to Rebecca, but she should've been more considerate with her response. If I wanted to chat about Mallory, then I would have. But I didn't owe her and Dan access to the pain Mallory caused me. Not when I didn't even know what it all meant.

Chris Bedell

"I'd rather not think about Mallory," I said. "She's already caused enough trouble for me, and I'll be damned if I let her live rent free in my head."

Rebecca tucked her hands into her pockets. "It's okay if you're pissed about Mallory being released. Anger only makes you human."

"I have nothing to be angry about," I said.

Dan frowned at me. "You don't have to put on an act for our sake."

I made a brief fist. "Fine. It fucking sucks that Mallory was released and I'm terrified about what she's gonna do next. Happy?"

"Want some advice?" Rebecca asked.

I snorted. "I've got a feeling you're gonna talk whether I wanna hear what you've gotta say or not."

"You're right about that," Dan said.

"Don't antagonize Mallory," Rebecca said. "You're entitled to feel whatever way you do. However, nothing good will come from reigniting your war with Mallory. Especially when you've got everything you want with Archie."

Rebecca had a point, despite how her positive attitude nauseated me. I had everything I wanted with Archie, and it'd be a shame for my relationship to go up in flames.

"I need to ask your advice about something, and I need to keep it vague," I said.

A curl whipped Rebecca's face while the wind continued roaring. "Not sure I like the sound of this," she said.

"Would you wanna know the truth if someone you loved did something terrible?" I asked.

Dan stopped walking before crossing his arms. "What the hell are you talking about?"

"I can't say anything more," I said.

Rebecca exhaled a deep breath. "Depends on why you wanna reveal the truth. Is it because you're trying to do the right thing or because you wanna cleanse your guilty conscience?"

25

Between Love and Death

My Adam's apple bobbed. "Can't it be both?"

"Then you use your best judgement," Rebecca said. "Anyway, we gotta pick up the pace or we'll never make the movie."

My shoulders twitched. Damn. I should've realized one conversation with Dan and Rebecca wouldn't fix what I did to Mallory. This was real life, not a movie. So, there weren't any easy solutions.

"We could always grab a bite to eat first, then see a later showing," Dan suggested.

"There's something else Dan and I wanted to say." Rebecca grabbed my arms. "We're really sorry about your mother. And if there's anything you need, then please don't hesitate to ask. You don't need to suffer in silence."

MONDAY, JUNE 17

Archie and I faced each other in my bed while we caught our breath. Mom was out with a friend, so we had the house to ourselves for the evening.

Archie smirked. "Something wrong?"

"No."

He winked. "I can tell when you're not being completely honest."

Fuck. My moment of reckoning arrived. And I would have to decide what I would tell Archie in the next few seconds.

"I'm fine," I lied. "Just happy we're getting the happy ending we deserve."

Yeah. I just couldn't find the courage to be honest with Archie about scheming against Mallory. Not because what Mom said was wrong—it wasn't. But because the vulnerability terrified me. Archie might not like the real me once he realized what I was capable of. So, I'd rather live a lie. Deception was simpler, really. I only hurt Mallory because I did what needed to be done to get her out of the way. So, it wasn't like I'd continue scheming against people—I wouldn't. I had no desire to

Chris Bedell

continue my manipulations. I also couldn't forget about how Mallory wasn't innocent. She was a schemer as much as I was. Like with her wanting Archie just because I rejected her. And in a way, Mallory brought everything on herself.

Archie chuckled. "Phew. You scared me for a moment."

"Sorry," I murmured.

Archie sat up in bed, then slid his boxers and shorts on in a matter of seconds. "We should think about what we wanna order for dinner. I'm fine with either sushi or pizza."

My heart fluttered. In a matter of seconds, I sealed my fate with Archie—I chose not to tell him the truth about Mallory. And now I'd have to live with the consequences. So, yeah, I'd have to start praying Mallory didn't have something terrible planned for me.

AFTER

SUNDAY, DECEMBER 8

I entered the visitor's room at the county jail.

I hurried towards the guy sporting an orange jumpsuit at the empty table. I gave him a quick kiss on the lips before hugging him. He pulled back from me after a beat, then we sat down at the table.

An awkward silence ensued while I continued gazing at him. Words couldn't describe the joy from how good it felt to love someone who wasn't Archie or Mallory. I was human like everyone else and deserved someone who cared about me.

I smiled. "Good to see you, Ezra."

"What the hell are you doing here?" he asked.

"I'm not gonna abandon you just because I was released from prison."

He scoffed. "You took a big risk by hugging and kissing me. Usually, physical contact isn't allowed in the visitor's room."

"You see those men?" I pointed to the guards by the door. "Gemma bribed them so he'd look the other way during our embrace."

"Lovely."

I raised an eyebrow. "What's gotten into you? I thought you'd be happier to see me."

"What you did was wrong, Chad."

My stomach clenched. Ezra needed to lose his judgmental tone ASAP. I never said I was perfect. I also hadn't killed two people like Mallory—well, three people if I counted Kelly. But who did or didn't murder Kelly was a problem for another day.

"I'm doing what I need to do," I said through gritted teeth.

Ezra shook his head. "Revenge is more important than our relationship?"

"Please don't put words in my mouth. I wouldn't be visiting you if I didn't care about you."

"One visit is hardly life changing."

I leaned closer, and my elbows slid onto the table. "You really gonna chastise me because I did what was necessary for my freedom?"

"You chose revenge over me."

I huffed. "How would you feel if you were framed for a murder you didn't commit and were then burned with a cigarette lighter and nearly beaten to death?"

Ezra bit his lip. "I was there for you when that happened."

Ezra might not have raised his voice, but he still shouldn't have said what he had. Didn't matter if one day passed or a thousand days passed. I'd never forget how Ezra was there during the darkest time of my life. Mom's death had nothing on being almost beaten to death and tortured with a lit cigarette lighter. That type of violence was something nobody should experience. Not now. Not ever. So, Ezra didn't need to remind me of that day.

I placed my hands on my lap. "I know, and I'm thankful for that."

"You shouldn't have come," Ezra said.

My shoulders tensed. "I'm not gonna let you push me away."

Yeah. I meant what I said. Despite the unconventional way of meeting, Ezra was the one good thing in my life. Something Mallory didn't know about, something she couldn't take from me. And when I finished with Mallory, Ezra and I would have our happily ever after. I didn't know how, but we would. It was what we deserved after everything we went through.

Ezra's eyes widened, accentuating their menacing green color. "Too late for that."

"What do you want from me?" I demanded.

"I just wanna be with you."

"And you can be. I'll keep visiting."

He snickered. "Unless you get distracted by your new priorities."

"I've got time for both."

"Easier said than done." Ezra remained silent for a moment while his chest rose and fell. "I'm in jail for a robbery I didn't commit, and you were the only good thing in my life."

"I'll work to clear you once I've finished my mission."

Ezra looked down at the table. "And to think I..."

"What?" I snapped, rage shooting through me faster. I didn't understand Ezra's current contempt. Life could be good again—Ezra just needed to have some patience. I had no reason to lie to him.

"Forget it," he mumbled.

I glanced over Ezra, including his spiked black hair. It'd be so nice if one thing could go right. This visit was supposed to bring me joy—not give me heartache. But no. The universe had other plans, and I'd have to deal with Ezra reverting back to his previously jaded personality.

"Were you gonna tell me you love me?" I asked.

"Doesn't matter. Just go."

I squeezed his hand. "Everything will be fine."

"Doubtful."

My mouth opened, yet words escaped me. For once, I didn't have the perfect comeback. Having a comfort response would've been nice. But I didn't wanna risk alienating Ezra any further. Not when my current standing with him was already dubious.

Chris Bedell

"I've never let myself be so vulnerable before," Ezra continued.

"Someone hasn't threatened you, have they?" I asked.

"Not yet. Somehow, nobody knows what I'm in jail for."

I continued rubbing his hand. "Just keep being careful. I'd hate to see anything bad happen to you."

"This is gonna be the last time we talk. I don't want you to visit, write, or call. Understand?"

I shook my head. "You don't mean that."

"Guard!" Ezra exclaimed.

One of the guards by the door walked over to our table, then grabbed Ezra. The guard led Ezra to the exit before leaving the visitor's room. The door slammed shut and Ezra was now gone.

My heart beat faster. I prayed this conversation with Ezra wouldn't be the last words we ever said to each other. Because I didn't know what I'd do if an unpleasant conversation was the last memory I had of Ezra.

MONDAY, DECEMBER 9

I stood in the kitchen, drinking a cup of coffee while afternoon sunlight poked through the window. Gemma was out shopping at the local mall, so I was alone with my thoughts. More specifically, how my house would never be the same now that Mom was dead.

The doorbell rang several times, and I placed the mug on the counter before exiting the kitchen and opening the front door.

"What the fuck are you doing here?" I asked after opening the front door.

Archie tucked his hands into his jacket pockets while his teeth chattered. "Can I come in? It'll only take a minute."

"Fine." I gesticulated at him, and closed the front door after Archie entered the house.

He tilted his head. "Gemma isn't home?"

"No, you're fine."

31

Between Love and Death

"Good."

I glared at him. "You're the one who sought me out."

"Mallory woke up from surgery."

"Great."

"She hasn't said anything to anyone of us," Archie said.

My eyebrows inched up. "Did the police talk to her?"

"Not yet. Her doctor turned them away."

"Fantastic."

Archie pressed his hands together. "I owe you an apology, man."

"For what?" I asked.

Yeah. Archie was going have to be more specific. I wasn't a mind reader, and there were a lot of things he could've wanted to atone for. Like for not forgiving me after discovering I framed Mallory for killing Tommy. Or not supporting me while I was in jail awaiting trial. Or even not caring about Mom dying.

His jaw twitched. "I shouldn't have asked you if you were sleeping with Gemma. That was wrong of me, and I'm sorry."

I snorted. "No shit."

"No offense, but you could try being civil. I didn't have to drop by, but I did. And you wanna know why? Because I care about doing the right thing."

I crossed my arms. "Being you must be great."

"Excuse me?"

"You heard me."

He exhaled a breath. "If you're pissed about something, then out with it."

"Life is more complicated than always caring about doing the right thing." I fought back tears while the events of the last fourteen months replayed in my mind. Crying couldn't happen in front of Archie. Not after everything that transpired between us. Archie couldn't see me in such a fragile state. He'd already stolen enough from me when he chose Mallory over me. "And it'd be nice if someone cared about what I went

Chris Bedell

through. Like how being framed for a murder I didn't commit subsequently caused me to get burned with a cigarette lighter and almost beaten to death. And we can't forget about my mother dying before I was released. So, you know what? Spare me the self-righteous hypocrisy."

Archie grunted. "I'm sorry about jail and your mother dying. You didn't deserve that."

"No shit."

"Revenge isn't the answer," Archie said, raising his voice. "You deserve happiness, and I hope you find it."

"Just empty words."

"What do you want from me?" Archie spat.

I stepped forward, so close that my breath might've tickled Archie's skin. I then straightened Archie's collar. "You're jealous."

Archie blinked. "Huh."

I cackled. "When you commented about whether or not Gemma and I were sleeping together, you really meant to say you wish you were sleeping with me."

"Don't be ridiculous."

"Wanna know something, Arch?" I asked. "I've moved on from you with a new guy, Ezra. We met in jail. And we're gonna get our happy ending when I'm finished with Mallory. But if you apologize, then I might consider going easy on you. Mallory is the real target."

"Bullshit." He locked eyes with me, so long that I wondered if he was gonna kiss me. "Our relationship is the last thing on my mind."

"Keep telling yourself that."

Archie beamed his eyes. "Here's the real truth. When you comment about me wanting to kiss you, you're referring to how you secretly wanna kiss me."

Wow. Archie must've changed more than I realized in my absence. I never once thought Archie would be capable of a comeback.

"Don't be silly, babe. You mean nothing to me," I said.

33

Between Love and Death

"Keep telling yourself that."

My scowl intensified—Archie had to know I wasn't the same innocent kid who was framed for murder. "We done here?"

"Yeah." Archie shuffled towards the front door, then exited my house without another word.

TUESDAY, DECEMBER 10

Gemma and I sat on the living room couch, enjoying Cosmos.

Gemma put her drink on the wooden living room table before resuming eye contact. "Not trying to upset you, but you should've been smarter about Archie."

"How so?" I sipped my Cosmo, letting the cranberry flavor linger on my tongue before swallowing it.

"We're gonna need him for the plan."

I gave Gemma a look. "Do I even wanna know what you're gonna say next?"

"You're gonna skate on the Mallory thing. And when you do, you've gotta be ready for what's next."

I adjusted my posture, sitting up straighter. "And what's that?"

"Getting closer to Archie, start sleeping with him, and then arrange for Mallory to catch you. You'll dump Archie soon after getting him to care about you. Then, you'll move onto Mallory. I can get you sedatives so you can drug Mallory."

"Okay…"

"Giving Mallory sleeping pills will make her blackout, lose time, and seem mentally ill again. And then she'll be locked up at the sanitarium again."

I stroked my chin. Creepy. It was as if Gemma and I shared a brain. I vaguely remembered making a similar comment to Mom when Mallory was released from the mental hospital back in June.

34

Interesting. Perhaps Gemma and I had more in common than I realized. It took a certain type of person to concoct such a twisted plan.

"I'm in," I said.

"Good. I'd hate for you to suddenly grow a conscience."

I pouted. "Only one problem. Archie is gonna be pissed at me because of our previous fight."

She giggled. "Not a big deal. Just say your emotions got the best of you. Nobody would question your current grief."

Color me impressed. Gemma had an answer for everything, and I didn't know what I'd do if Gemma wasn't in my life. She was the answer to all my problems. So, with her help, Mallory would be left with nothing. And I'd be left with everything.

"I also got into an argument with Ezra when I visited him the other day," I said. "Probably hates me and is gonna go back to being a dick."

She patted my knee. "You can also blame that conversation on your grief. I'm sure Ezra would love for you to give him a reason to forgive you."

"True."

Gemma rubbed her hands together. "We're gonna need refills on the Cosmos."

"You're a bad influence."

"Be glad you don't have to attend school anymore since you're 18."

Yup. Gemma was serious about what she said. Since I was legally an adult, I had no plans of resuming my education. Not when I needed to devote all my time to destroying Mallory. There was also nothing left for me at school.

THURSDAY, DECEMBER 12

I entered Mallory's hospital room mid-morning, and she quickly rolled her eyes at me.

Between Love and Death

I couldn't help my current déjà vu, though. This current moment reminded me of that day last April when I visited Mallory at the sanitarium—Mallory sported the same scornful look then that she did now.

"What are you doing here?" she asked.

I walked over to Mallory's bed after checking and making sure her door was locked. I would be damned if I let someone interrupt this conversation.

"The police haven't come to arrest me," I said.

"You have me to thank for that."

"How so?"

Mallory sat up in her bed, then fluffed her pillow. "I told them I was fooling around with a gun and the whole thing was an accident."

"That's very big of you."

Mallory leaned closer to me. "Don't get too carried away with praising me. I was being slightly selfish. There's no fun in letting you go to jail. Not when I'd rather finish you off myself."

"This is war?"

She picked her nail. "Like you didn't know that when you stepped foot inside here."

"True."

"But give it your best shot. It'll make crushing you more fun."

My pulse quickened. This was it—Mallory and I were really gonna go through with our war. So, I'd just have to hope I'd win. Failure wasn't an option when so much was at stake.

36

BEFORE

FRIDAY, JUNE 21

I banged on Mallory and Kelly's front door while gray clouds remained clumped together in the sky. The weather forecast mentioned something about bad weather today, but it hadn't so much as rained yet.

The door opened, revealing Kelly.

She glared at me. "If you're looking for Mallory, she isn't home. Mallory went to the beach. But I can give her a message if you don't feel like waiting."

My lips curled. "Cut the bullshit."

"Excuse me?"

"Can I come inside or what?"

Kelly threw a gaze inside, then I entered her home. She locked the door behind me before turning around to face me in a matter of seconds.

She put her hands on her hips. "I've been wondering if you'd stop by for a chat."

"You've got a lot of explaining to do."

"I imagine you aren't happy about Mallory being released from the sanitarium."

Between Love and Death

Please. There was no need for Kelly to state the obvious. Even people living on remote islands in the South Pacific would know I wasn't pleased about Mallory's second chance. It wasn't like I asked for a lot. I just wanted a chance at a good future with Archie.

"You should've told me what was going on," I said.

Her eyebrows scrunched. "Why would I do you any favors?"

"Because we're partners in crime."

She pushed a lock of hair to the side. "Hardly. I only helped you because you pressured me into it."

"You had no right hiring Mallory a lawyer. What was so hard about keeping her locked up in the sanitarium indefinitely?"

"For a murder she didn't commit?" Kelly asked.

Kelly needed a reality check, like yesterday. She couldn't have seriously thought Mallory was a good person. It didn't matter if Mallory invented a cure for cancer or solved world hunger. Mallory would always be evil because of the things she did to me during the previous school year. I also wasn't Mallory's family. So, I wasn't obligated to forgive Mallory for anything. Not even if she got on her knees and begged.

I pushed my sleeves up. "We've had this discussion already. Mallory's innocence regarding Tommy doesn't absolve her of other sins."

"She blackmailed me," Kelly blurted.

My gaze constricted. "Come again?"

"So, maybe you should think twice before you judge me."

"What did she blackmail you with?" I asked.

"For being Tommy's real killer, and there's only one way she could've discovered the truth."

Sweat dripped down my face. If Kelly had something to say, then she needed to say it. Leaving me in suspense was rude. Having a good idea about what she was getting at didn't mean I was right. There was a chance I was wrong.

38

"How could you betray me?" Kelly asked, stepping closer.

"I don't know what you're implying."

"Please. I know you visited Mallory at the sanitarium in April, so don't deny it."

I took in several deep breaths. "Not like I wanted to double-cross you."

"Doesn't matter. I'm now at Mallory's mercy because of you. So, I hope you're happy."

"I never wanted to hurt you," I said.

"Too late. You already did."

I started pacing back and forth in our current spot a few feet away by the front door. "There's gotta be something we can do."

Kelly frowned. "You're on your own because I'm done with scheming."

"She could expose the truth to Archie," I stammered.

"That's your problem, not mine."

More anger shot through my veins. Perhaps Kelly had more in common with Mallory than she realized. I never once considered that Kelly could be as cruel as Mallory. Then again, they were sisters. So, they had to have some shared similarities—whether they admitted it or not.

"Since when have you and Mallory gotten so close?" I asked.

She put her hands behind her neck. "I'm doing what I have to do to survive. Kind of like what you did when you framed her for Tommy's murder."

"A little sympathy would be nice," I said.

Her shoulders shuddered. "What do you want me to say?"

"That you'll help me take down Mallory once and for all."

"Have you been paying attention to anything I've been saying?" Kelly dashed to the front door, then opened it. "Now please, leave. I have a headache, and you've only managed to make it worse."

39

Between Love and Death

I made a fist while tears dotted my eyes. Maybe, just maybe, genuine emotion would convince Kelly to help me. I had nothing left to lose. "You've gotta help me. I've got nobody," I said.

"If you want this to end, then you're gonna have to tell Archie the truth about everything. It's the only way to move past this."

I grimaced. No explanation necessary about how Kelly's advice was terrible. I already tried telling Archie the truth, and that didn't work. So, I needed to think of a solution fast if I didn't want my relationship with Archie to implode.

TUESDAY, JUNE 25

I entered the kitchen after having a Starbucks date with Archie, discovering Mallory and Mom chatting.

I gasped. "The fuck are you doing here?"

Mallory sighed at me. "I just wanted to stop and check in on your mother. Cancer is no laughing matter—I had an uncle die of it a few years ago."

My attention shifted to Mom. "You shouldn't have let Mallory in the house."

"Coffee is harmless."

I cocked my head, hoping Mom was wrong. But no. Two coffee cups were on the kitchen counter next to Mom and Mallory.

"You're coming with me." I raced towards Mallory before grabbing her arm and dragging her away.

Normally, I'd never man-handle someone. But Mallory was the exception to the rule. She needed to know it wasn't okay for her to drop by—whether announced or unannounced.

I closed the front door behind her, then stared her down. "You have no right involving my mother in our feud."

Mallory licked her lips. "If you wanted to play rough, then all you had to do was ask."

40

"Please. As if I'd ever sleep with you again."

"Stranger things have happened."

I screamed. "Enough bullshit! Tell me why you really stopped by."

"I wasn't lying. I wanted to pay my respects to your mom."

I leaned forward, brushing my lips against Mallory's right ear. "We both know what you're doing, and it isn't gonna work."

"Oh, yeah? And what's that?"

"You're trying to get me wound up with passive aggressive actions so I look like the crazy one." I took in a deep breath. "But it's not gonna work. This isn't last year, and I'm five steps ahead of you."

My bravado was necessary, despite my pulse hammering in my ears. Mallory couldn't know I was afraid of her. If she did, then she'd take advantage of the opportunity and destroy my life.

She laughed. "You're doing a good job of looking like a nut-job all on your own. Dragging me out of the kitchen unprovoked isn't normal behavior."

"Don't get cute."

"Tell me something," she said. "How's the romance with Archie? Is it as passionate as ever?"

"Shut the fuck up. You don't know a fucking thing about my love for Archie."

"Careful. There you again looking like the jaded one."

"Not too late to tell me what you want. Maybe we can work something out."

Rain pattered against the ground, then purple tinged lightning lit up the sky. Thunder howled while I continued looking into Mallory's eyes. Just because she didn't have a menacing look on her face didn't mean she had pure intentions.

"The only thing I want is for you to have a good day." Mallory walked down the front steps and towards her car, leaving me to my thoughts.

Between Love and Death

My heart lurched. My gut instinct had to have been right. Mallory had to have been playing nice as part of some bigger plan. I sent her to a sanitarium for a crime she didn't commit and there was no getting over that. I would've been consumed with rage if I were in her position. Nothing fair about being blamed for a crime I wasn't guilty of.

FRIDAY, JUNE 28

Archie rolled off my back, and sweat soon dripped down our faces. Mom once again had plans with a friend, so we had the house to ourselves.

Archie turned, facing me. "We need to chat."

"Did I do something wrong?"

My comment might not have been the smartest thing in light of how I framed Mallory for something she didn't do, yet I couldn't help what I said. Mallory blabbed to Archie about what I did, and he was gonna breakup with me.

He chuckled. "You need to worry less."

"Have you met me?"

"It's about what you said earlier."

"Gonna have to be more specific."

"About man-handling Mallory when she visited your mom."

"Oh…"

"I'm not mad at you or anything. I just think you made the wrong move. It's like you completely disregarded what I said at Starbucks when we saw Mallory. If you continue showing your rage, then you're playing right into her hand."

"I can't help it. She has a talent for annoying me."

"Then you're gonna have to control your temper." Archie gave me a quick kiss on the lips. "You're better than she is, and you can't allow her to ruin your life."

"I know, I know."

His grin widened. "I'm only telling you this because I care."

"Thank you for not dumping me in light of what I told you about how I handled Mallory. Some people wouldn't be so kind."

Archie snickered louder. "Do you really think I'd dump you because you made a silly mistake?"

I remained silent. For once, I didn't know what to say. Being nice and being forgiving were two different things. There was no guarantee that Archie would wanna continue dating me once he realized what I did to Mallory.

"Shit," Archie continued. "Maybe I'm not as great of a boyfriend as I thought I was. I don't want you to be uncomfortable with me, because you really can tell me anything. Promise not to judge."

I swallowed. "Good to know."

Fuck. Whether Archie realized it or not, he just gave me an opportunity to be honest about what I did to Mallory. Yet I, once again, behaved like a coward by keeping the truth from him. So, I was just gonna have to continue praying Archie would never know Mallory didn't kill Tommy. Hope was just the only thing I had left.

Archie eyed me. "Wanna order a pizza?"

I winked. "Don't wanna go for round two?"

"What's gotten into you, babe?"

My cheeks burned. "I can't help it. I'm just so lucky to have you."

He ruffled my hair. "Good to know you care."

Please. Archie didn't just say what he did. Anyone with half a brain could tell my feelings for him were real. I wouldn't have schemed so hard against Mallory if they weren't real. So, yeah, more uneasiness rolled through my stomach. If I wasn't careful, then casual moments like this conversation with Archie would be a thing of the past. Mallory's good girl routine could only last for so long. I just knew it.

AFTER

FRIDAY, DECEMBER 19

The temperatures were in the sixties for the last couple of days, so I suggested that Archie and I sit on my front steps when he came over afterschool.

I cocked my head, then smiled. "Thanks for agreeing to meet."

"I'm not sure what we have to discuss after everything that transpired during our last conversation." He sighed. "But I'd be lying if I said I wasn't worried about you."

I choked. The universe couldn't have been generous enough to make Archie fall into my lap. Yet here I was, wondering why he'd be concerned about me. We weren't dating anymore, so Archie didn't owe me anything.

Deep breaths. I couldn't seem too eager about Archie. Then he'd know something was up. And I couldn't have that. Not if I wanted my plan to seduce and dump Archie and gaslight Mallory to work.

"Truthfully, I was gonna checkup on you." He rubbed my knee, sending chills up my back. I wouldn't have minded seeing Mallory's reaction to Archie being so touchy. "This is your first Christmas without your mother, and I can't imagine how you must be feeling."

44

Chris Bedell

My stomach sank while disbelief flooded my body. Somehow, I forgot about this Christmas being the first one without Mom. But maybe, just maybe, that was for the best. Loss didn't get better over time. It got worse. I'd always have to live with how Mom missed out on half of her life, which fucking sucked. Nobody should ever experience that type of cruelty.

"Thanks. I appreciate you being so considerate." My hands fell to my lap. "But I owe you an apology."

His eyebrows inched up. "For what?"

"The things I said during our last conversation. I'm not gonna pretend to be a good person and forgive Mallory. But you didn't deserve the things I said, and I wanted you to know I'm sorry."

"Apology accepted."

"Really?" I asked.

"Yeah. I mean, I wish you didn't have this feud with Mallory. Although, you're an adult, and I can't tell you how to behave."

I snickered. "True."

Archie nudged me. "You must be glad Mallory isn't gonna press charges."

"I don't wanna discuss Mallory."

"Fair enough."

The image of Mom once again flashed through my mind. More specifically, last Christmas. I couldn't believe that last year's Christmas was my last Christmas with Mom. Somehow, that seemed like a lifetime ago. Not wanting to be exposed for Tommy's murder was my biggest priority then, not if Mom would still be alive a year from now.

Tears welled in my eyes. I was barely an adult, so it was only natural for me to be emotional. I'd challenge anyone not to be devastated if they were in my position. It wasn't like I wanted to cry to manipulate Archie. Using something to my advantage was one thing, but I wasn't completely comfortable with Archie. Not when he was still dating Mallory.

45

Archie looked into my eyes, then wiped a tear from my cheek. "What is it?"

I scratched the side of my head. "It's dumb."

"Promise not to judge?"

"Forever is a long time when you're only eighteen. Just don't know how I'm supposed to live the rest of my life without my mother."

"I know, I know." Archie pulled me in for a hug before I could so much as blink. I sobbed into his chest while he rubbed my back for a good ten or fifteen seconds.

We detached from our embrace, then stole a gaze with each other. Our glance lingered for a beat. Before I knew it, we were kissing each other. Both of us equally responsible since we made to move at the same time.

I couldn't lie to myself, though. Not this time. Every neuron in my body became electrified while Archie and I made out. There was just something intoxicating about his tongue in my mouth while inhaling the fruity and earthy scent of whatever deodorant he wore. His fingers moved to my cheeks, tracing the contours of my face while the kissing grew deeper and harder.

Archie pulled away. "Fuck."

"Sorry," I mumbled.

"That shouldn't have happened. I'm dating Mallory."

I rolled my eyes so hard it was a miracle they didn't pop out of my head. "Never stopped you before."

He gave me a look.

Shit. Insulting Archie might not have been the right thing to do if I didn't wanna alienate myself. Yet I couldn't help myself. A part of Archie must've enjoyed how Mallory and I were both attracted to him. Wanting to be loved and desired only made him human. It wasn't like he intentionally behaved like a fuckboy. I hoped not, at least.

"Sorry," I whispered.

Chris Bedell

"Don't apologize on my account." He grabbed his mug, which was on the step above his leg, then sipped his coffee. "I have waffled between you and Mallory, and I know it isn't fair."

"You can't tell her about the kiss," I said.

"I'm not an idiot."

"I'm serious, Archie. You've got no idea what Mallory would do if she discovered you were stepping out on her."

"It's not like we had sex," Archie said.

I chuckled. "Not yet, anyway."

"We're not gonna have sex. Not now, not ever." Archie bit his nail. "Too much has happened between us. But that doesn't mean we can't be friends. I'd be lying if I said I didn't want you in my life."

I averted my gaze, focusing on a squirrel darting across my front lawn. "Good to know."

He clapped my knee. "And you're with Ezra now."

"Don't know about that."

"What the fuck are you talking about?" he asked.

"We had a fight, and I haven't visited him since."

"I'm sure you guys can work it out if you care about him. You don't deserve to be miserable for the rest of your life."

Archie reached for his mug, then finished his coffee. "I'm serious, Chad. You're a great guy, and someone is gonna see that one day."

My heart almost skipped a beat. I couldn't help lingering on the "great guy" part of Archie's comment. I wasn't psychic, but perhaps a small part of Archie still had romantic feelings for me. Even if he didn't wanna admit it. So maybe, just maybe, he stopped the kiss because that was the right thing to do. Not because he wanted to.

"Why don't we change the subject?" he asked.

I nodded.

"Why don't you spend Christmas with my sister, parents, and me?" Archie looped his arms around me. "You shouldn't be alone on Christmas."

Between Love and Death

"What about Mallory?" I asked.

He looked away from me. "She's going out of town for a few days."

"Great. I love being a backup."

He whipped his head back and forth. "You aren't my backup. Honestly, Mallory and I wouldn't be spending Christmas together even if she were in town."

I exploded into laughter. "Good to know."

Archie gave me a pleading look. "Promise me that you'll think about it?"

"I don't wanna be a charity case."

"That's not how I see you—I genuinely enjoy your company," Archie said.

Yeah. My theory about Archie possibly still having feelings for me had to be correct. The fact that we could fall into a comfortable closeness—such as spending time with his sister and parents—counted for something. He probably wouldn't invite Rebecca and Dan to do the same thing.

Archie looked at his watch on is right hand. "I should go."

"No problem."

He stood, then cracked a smile. "Thanks for the coffee."

"Don't mention it." I downed the rest of my coffee. "Anyway, drive home safely."

Archie descended the front steps and arrived at his car in a matter of seconds. I couldn't help doing what I always did when I was confused – dwell on something. More specifically, his offer about Christmas. I couldn't deny how his proposition touched me—some people wouldn't be as considerate as him. So, his kindness was something even if he continued associating with Mallory.

I couldn't accept Archie's offer, though. Not because I no longer wanted to get close to Archie and abandon my revenge mission. I didn't. But because I couldn't allow myself to be vulnerable in front of Archie's

48

MONDAY, DECEMBER 23

I sat at a table in back of Café Tomorrow while I kept looking over my shoulder.

I was supposed to meet someone, but the person hadn't arrived. And I was close to leaving. Being patient and compassionate were one thing. But I hated how some people loved wasting other people's time. That was pretty disrespectful.

The sign clanked against the door when it opened. Footsteps shuffled against the ground, then the girl sat across from me.

She bit her lip. "Sorry. Got stuck in traffic."

My eyes bulged. "This meeting was your idea, Mallory."

"I know, I know. But I'm really not lying about the traffic. You can check the traffic reports on the radio if you don't believe me." Mallory took off her coat and scarf before placing them on the back of her chair.

"You can't jerk me around," I bellowed.

She made a clicking noise with her tongue. "I know, and it won't happen again. Although, you're gonna wanna hear what I have to say."

"And why is that?" I demanded.

"Because I wanna call a truce." Mallory flipped her hair over her shoulders. "You lost your mother. I lost my sister. So, I think we've suffered enough."

I plucked a loose eyelash. "You're trying to trap me into a false sense of security before you take one final wrecking ball to my life."

Her chest expanded and contracted while she forced in a gulp of air. If I didn't know better, then I would've guessed she was struggling with what she was gonna say next. Almost as if a small part of her was still human. "Not this time. I just wanna enjoy life," she said.

I begrudgingly bobbed my head at her. "Fine. We can have a truce or whatever."

Her eyes lit up. "Really?"

"Yup."

She extended her hand. "Shake on it?"

"Why the hell not?" I shook her hand.

Mallory gripped my hand so hard she might as well have broken it. Yet that didn't matter. I was beating her at her own game. Having her believe we weren't enemies was the fastest way to get Mallory to let her guard down.

Her jaw trembled. "Hope you're doing okay in light of this being the first Christmas without your mother."

I wiggled my eyebrows. "I'm more interested in you. Rumor has it you're gonna be out of town for a few days."

Accepting her truce didn't mean I couldn't be sassy. Mallory still had to know she couldn't push me around. So, it was good that I reminded her of how I knew something about her life. I could lurk in the shadows ready to pounce just like she was the first day of junior year when she spied on my conversation with Archie.

"Yeah, I've got a few things to take care of." She wrapped her pearl necklace around her fingers, twisting it tighter and tighter. "Wait. How do you know I'm going away for a few days?"

"A little birdie told me," I said.

She let go of her necklace. "Whatever. Just hope you enjoy Christmas."

FRIDAY, DECEMBER 27

I sat on the living room couch while enjoying a cup of coffee. Something vibrated in my pocket, so I grabbed my iPhone. I had a call from a number I didn't recognize, but I accepted the call. No telling what was and wasn't important these days.

50

Chris Bedell

"Hello?" I said.

"This is Warden Jones of the county jail," said the man.

"How can I help you?"

He coughed, creating brief static on his end of the line. "I'm sorry to have to tell you this, but I am contacting you to inform you that Ezra Kingsley died earlier today. He was stabbed in the shower with a shiv."

Getting shot would've hurt less than what the warden just said. It didn't matter how obvious the idea sounded. Life could change in an instant. Sometimes for the better. Sometimes for the worse. I couldn't have heard Warden Jones correctly. Ezra couldn't be dead. Not before I visited him and mended our relationship.

"Come again?" I asked, sweat dripping down my back.

"Ezra Kingsley is dead, and I'm truly sorry for your loss. Dying at eighteen is a tragedy."

I hung up on the warden, then tossed my iPhone onto the couch.

I screamed. Gemma was at the mall, so I didn't have to worry about her seeing me in such a vulnerable state. Purging my feelings was also the healthy thing to do. I'd just never be okay with how unfair life was. First Mom died. And now Ezra. Fuck. The universe really was a cruel motherfucker.

The doorbell rang, but I didn't get up. Whoever it was would leave a note if it was that important.

I put my hand in my lap and cried. And cried. And cried. I just didn't understand why one fucking thing couldn't go right. I wasn't asking for diamonds or a mansion. I only wanted a chance at a future.

The doorbell rang several more times.

Shit. I was gonna have to answer the door. If the person pressed the doorbell several times, then they weren't gonna go away.

I heaved out a sigh, then stood. I shuffled towards the front door before opening it a moment later. My heart almost leapt out of my chest. It was Archie.

"What are you doing here?" I asked.

Between Love and Death

He shoved his hands into his pockets. "Just wanted to check up on you. In case you were feeling down about your mother."

I didn't respond. Instead, I stared at him with a blank expression. Even a famous writer would've been at a loss of words if they in my position. Some clever phrase or speech couldn't encompass the random cruelty of life.

"Can I come in?" he asked.

I nodded, then closed the door behind him.

He lifted my chin, making the hairs on my back rise. My desire for revenge didn't change that I was human. Like how I might've been weak for Archie. "What's going on?" he asked.

I shrieked. "Ezra's dead ... someone stabbed him."

His jaw lowered. "I'm so sorry."

Archie pulled me in for a hug and I didn't stop him.

I wailed into his chest, muffling my screams. The universe's sense of humor was beyond fucked. It gave me another opportunity to bond with Archie, but it was at Ezra's expense.

I pulled back, then kissed Archie before I could change my mind. And Archie didn't stop me, which was great. Only one thing was certain–I didn't wanna drown in the loneliness and emptiness. And something good needed to come from Ezra's death, so no harm in using this moment to further my agenda.

I wasn't a monster. I was human. I could be both devastated about Ezra's death and wanna escalate my mission. The ideas weren't mutually exclusive. And the only question was if Archie and I were gonna do more than kissing.

52

BEFORE

TUESDAY, JULY 2

I was about to make brownies—while Mom napped upstairs in her bedroom—when someone knocked on my front door several times. I rolled my eyes before exiting the kitchen and answering the front door. Making the brownies without being interrupted would've been nice. But no. The universe had other plans for me.

"What are you doing here?" I asked.

The vein on Archie's head surfaced. "Can I come in?"

"Sure," I said, nodding.

Archie entered my home, then I locked the door behind him. Unfortunately, the tense look on Archie's face hadn't disappeared. So yeah, I couldn't help the nervousness trembling through my body. If I didn't know better, a part of me suspected Mallory told Archie everything I did to her.

One. Two. Three. Four. Five. Six. Seven. Eight. Nine. Ten. Taking a few seconds to pause was the right thing to do. I couldn't allow myself to accidentally confess what I did in the event that Mallory hadn't told Archie the truth.

I pushed a lock of Archie's hair to the side. "What's going on, baby?"

Between Love and Death

"Mallory and I chatted yesterday."

Shit. My life was over and there wasn't a damn thing I could do about it. So, I was gonna have to figure out how I'd weasel out of what I did to Mallory. There just had to be a way out of my predicament. I refused to believe my relationship with Archie was over. Plenty of questionable people got happy endings—both in television shows and in real life—so I should've been no different. I still had no desire to intentionally hurt people. I just needed to do whatever it took to protect my future with Archie.

Archie pushed my hand away. "She told me everything. Like how you punched her on Sunday. She even has the black eye to prove it."

Okay. Deep breaths. My future with Archie wasn't over. Yet I still needed a second to understand what Archie just revealed. I was at home all of Sunday, so I couldn't have attacked her. Oh my god. Mallory must've injured herself, or coaxed Kelly or someone else into attacking her. Those were the only logical explanations I could think of. But if Mallory really concocted this phony story, then she was a crazier bitch than I realized.

"She's lying," I spat.

Archie furrowed is brow. "Can anyone account for your whereabouts on Sunday?"

"I didn't realize I needed an alibi."

"I'm not kidding around, Chad. This is serious, and you're lucky she didn't go to the police—I would've."

My eyebrows knitted together. "You think I'm capable of attacking Mallory?"

"You dragged her out of your house quite forcefully," Archie said.

"I was honest with you about that."

"I want you to tell me the truth right now!" he exclaimed.

"I was at home for all of Sunday. And I'd have you check with my mother, but she was out with friends the entire day." I looked Archie up and down. We couldn't have been having this conversation. Being

54

Chris Bedell

boyfriends meant we were supposed to trust each other. So, Mallory shouldn't have been able to poke doubt in our relationship.

He cackled. "Lovely. Just what I wanted to hear."

I lunged closer. "I need to know if you trust me, Archie. Seems like you're looking for any excuse to bail."

Regret didn't pang through my body even though it should've. I couldn't help myself with my remark. I just didn't know what got into Archie. He couldn't have been stupid enough to believe Mallory.

"You're the one who framed Mallory for murder," Archie said.

I fanned myself with my tee-shirt while more sweat clung to my body. "For a murder she was responsible for."

Archie remained silent while a weird look remained on his face.

"It'd be nice if you took my side," I said.

His jaw shook. "It's not that I don't wanna believe you. It's just that your hatred for Mallory is an open secret. Maybe you didn't mean to hurt her and simply lost your temper. I wouldn't hate you if that were the case."

Making excuses about my guilt wasn't enough. Someone still should've given Archie a soap opera slap. He should've been certain of my innocence. It was what I would've done if the situation were reversed.

"Mallory's lying," I said.

He patted my shoulder. "Fine. I believe you."

Archie should've responded with more conviction. The tone in his voice didn't inspire confidence.

I'd have to take what I could get, though. I had bigger problems than whether or not Archie trusted me. My debacle only had one solution. Go directly to the source no matter how difficult or awkward accosting Mallory might be. The only question was when and where Mallory and

55

I would have our confrontation.

MONDAY, JULY 8

I walked down the street while sunlight glinted against the sidewalk.

I hadn't dealt with Mallory's lie yet—going to her house seemed like the wrong move because she'd probably spin the situation. I also didn't wanna act on impulse and emotion. Acting irrationally could make the issue messier.

It was do or die. Mallory just exited a shop a few feet away from me, and I was gonna have to do something.

Mallory craned her neck. "Hi, Chad."

"You've got some nerve, bitch!"

So much for restraint. I couldn't help myself when it came to Mallory, though. She made me wanna kick or punch something. It felt like my feud with her was never gonna end no matter what I did.

"I know what you did," I said.

She waggled her eyebrows. "And what's that?"

"You told Archie I attacked you, which couldn't be further from the truth."

"I did no such thing," Mallory said.

"Enough. I'm not a complete moron!" I exclaimed.

Mallory giggled. "Could've fooled me."

"What did you just say?" I demanded.

"Nothing." Mallory remained silent for a minute or two before grabbing my hands. "I'd never lie to Archie about you, so he must be mistaken. Maybe he might need some time at the sanitarium. Could be for the best."

This girl was something else. First, she blabbed to Archie about something I didn't do and now she wanted to convince me that my boyfriend was crazy. Alright, then. Apparently, there was a first time for everything. At this point I wasn't sure what her goal was other than creating chaos. She was gonna have to try harder if she wanted to ruin my relationship with Archie. We came too far to let our relationship end over some trashy interloper.

I pointed to her face. "How'd you get the black eye?"

She didn't even so much as stutter. "I fell down the stairs while carrying my laundry basket. Kelly can vouch for me."

"You're really gonna stand by how you didn't tell Archie I attacked you?" I asked.

"Yes, because it's the truth." Mallory's hair slapped her in the face after the wind rippled through the air. "We talked, but it was just because I wanted to stop and make sure he knew I didn't have bad intentions."

I leaned against Mallory's right ear. "You're on very thin ice, so I'd be careful if I were you. Understand?"

Mallory's tongue wet her lips. "Was that a threat? Just wanna make sure I understand your intentions so I don't misrepresent them to Archie."

"I got rid of you once, and I could do the same again. Watch me," I said.

She pushed me aside. "Have fun with that."

THURSDAY, JULY 11

I returned from a quick trip to Starbucks, discovering Mom sitting on our front steps. I flashed Mom a smile. We were gonna have to have this talk no matter how painful of a subject Mallory was. No point in delaying it anymore.

"We need to chat." I sat down next to Mom. "Mallory didn't out my secret to Archie, but she is sewing chaos in our relationship."

Mom gulped more of her tea. "How so?"

"Doesn't matter." I tapped my feet against the step while a light drizzle fell against the ground. "Just gotta promise me one thing."

Between Love and Death

"And what's that?" Mom asked.

"You can't trust Mallory," I said. "There's no telling what she's capable of. So, please don't be fooled if she does something like drop by with cookies."

Mom pulled me against her body. "You're my son, so I'll always take your side regardless if I agree with you."

Relief washed over me. Nice to know one thing could go right. I didn't know what I would've done if Mom fought me. She was on borrowed time, and I didn't wanna spend her last days, weeks, or months fighting. Nothing good would come from bickering with her. Quarreling with her would only leave me with regret. And I already had enough of that.

I fought back tears. But not because of Mallory's antics or worrying about how my relationship with Archie was doomed. My mind remained focused on how Mom continued holding me—almost as if she didn't wanna let go. Death was inevitable no matter how much I loved Mom. There was gonna be a time when I wouldn't be able to touch her. And I'd just have to live with it like I did with everything else.

Mom glanced at me. "Something wrong, honey?"

I looked down at my knees. "Just want this moment to last forever."

"I know, I know," Mom said.

Creepy. Mom inferred what I meant without actually saying it. And said fact sucked. Mom didn't need to be worried about my feelings on top of everything else. She needed to stay alive for as long as possible.

AFTER

THURSDAY, JANUARY 2

Gemma and I sat at a table at the local mall's food court. She suggested an outing to get me out of the house and I didn't argue with her. I couldn't. And it was a miracle I even had the energy to get out of bed in the morning. One death was bad enough, but two pushed my limit. I didn't understand how I was supposed to live the rest of my life without Ezra. Especially since our last interaction was a fight.

Gemma rubbed my hand. "You can vent to me if you want. Promise not to judge you."

"I'm just so angry I didn't go back and visit Ezra." I slurped my soda. "What if Ezra died thinking nobody cared about him?"

"I'm sure that's not true," Gemma said.

"Should've swallowed my pride and visited him."

"Why didn't you?"

"I was afraid of allowing myself to be vulnerable. And I also wanted him to make the first move. Like calling me."

Gemma ate the last bite of her hamburger. "Why didn't you claim his body?"

"I have no rights. I'm not family, and we weren't married."

59

Between Love and Death

She smacked her head. "Sorry. Stupid question."

"Don't worry about it. It's not like it'll bring Ezra back—nothing will."

"At least you have your revenge to be focused on." Gemma shoved her tray to the side. "Speaking of which, you haven't given me any updates about that."

"Archie and I have been hanging out almost every day since Ezra died." I drummed my fingers against the table. "We even kissed a couple of times."

Gemma squealed. "That's great!"

"Not really. I have no idea what I'm doing because we haven't discussed the kisses."

"Don't overthink it."

I cocked my head to the left and then to the right—nobody was within earshot. "There's one thing we should discuss, though."

"What's up?" Gemma asked.

"How are we gonna drug Mallory with sedatives so she blacks outs, loses time, and people think she's mentally ill again?" I asked.

"You slip the sleeping pills into whatever she's eating or drinking."

I rolled my eyes. "I meant about how we're gonna get the sedatives. Not like I can see a doctor and get a prescription for sleeping pills. They'd be able to trace the pills back to me."

Yeah. I wasn't as obtuse as Mallory might've thought. If I was gonna go to such extremes to gaslight Mallory, then I'd have to leave no room for error. I refused to work so hard for destroying Mallory's life only to have my plan backfire.

"You've gotta stop worrying," Gemma said.

My scowl intensified. "Answer my question."

"I know a guy, but that's not important. You first gotta get Archie into bed, and arrange for Mallory to catch you."

When Gemma was right, she was right. Taking the plan one step at a time proved best—overthinking things would just drive me crazy. So

60

maybe, just maybe, the universe would throw a gift, and sleeping with Archie would be easier than it seemed. He was already halfway to cheating because of kissing me twice.

Gemma reached for my hand. "I also wanted to once again express my condolences. You don't deserve to be dealing with Ezra's death on top of everything else."

"Thank you," I forced out.

Gemma clenched her jaw. "I'll never force you to discuss anything you don't want to, but I'm always here for you. Hope you know that."

"Appreciate it."

Amusement would've overcome me if life weren't so morbid. If this were the beginning of junior year, then I would've been skeptical if someone told me Gemma would become my best friend. Yet here I was, plotting with Gemma as if it were as natural as breathing. And said fact was more than strange. Being close with Tommy's sister didn't seem right after what Tommy did. But Tommy was only a teenager when he died, so he hadn't deserved to die. Not completely.

My turn to hold Gemma's hand. "The same goes for you. I'm here if you wanna talk about Tommy."

A tear rolled down Gemma's cheek. "Feels like Tommy was never alive."

FRIDAY, JANUARY 3

Archie and I sat on my bed while moonlight poked through my bedroom curtains. Archie just closed the laptop. Biting my lip wasn't due to the movie we finished moments earlier being done. An intense look remained plastered on Archie's face—almost as if he wanted to talk to me about something.

"Something wrong?" I asked.

"We need to chat."

Between Love and Death

Wow. Perhaps I had a future as a psychic after all. I didn't wanna be right about Archie wanting to talk, yet I was. And I'd have to pray Archie wasn't mad at me because my revenge mission was the only thing I had left now that Mom and Ezra were dead.

The lump lingered in my throat. "What's up? Did I do something wrong?"

"The kisses can't happen again." Archie rested his hands on his lap. "I'm not gonna pretend I wasn't an equal participant. But I have a girlfriend, and cheating on her wouldn't be fair to either one of you."

"How noble," I quipped.

Archie caressed my head—like a parent would mess up their child's hair. "I still wanna be your friend, though."

"Even though I want revenge against Mallory?" I asked.

"Yes," he mumbled.

I gave him puppy dog eyes. "Why can't you end things with Mallory? You can't seriously believe Mallory is the love of your life?"

Yup. I could still ask a few questions despite how I had to be careful about not alienating myself. He admitted to being equally guilty as me with our making-out, so I was entitled to an answer about why we couldn't be together. It wasn't like I was being overly pushy about the subject. Archie might even get suspicious if I randomly lost interest in him after those two kisses.

"That would be cruel," Archie said.

"What do you even see in Mallory?" I demanded.

"She's fun."

I drew in a breath. "Did she even tell you where she was for the couple of days that she was out of town?"

"She doesn't have to account her whereabouts to me. Especially when I haven't been honest with her."

My lips quivered. "You better not tell her about our kisses. You've got no idea how complicated that would make life."

"Relax. I'm not idiot."

62

Chris Bedell

"Good." I rubbed his thigh. Not kissing him didn't mean I couldn't be suggestive. I could. So, I'd up the flirtation anyway I could. Nothing major. Just something to remind Archie that the spark still existed between us. "I know no thanks is necessary, but having your support with Ezra's death means a lot."

"Don't mention it," Archie said.

FRIDAY, JANUARY 10

I exited the Starbucks while the blue waned from the late afternoon sky. Pretty soon it'd be dark out.

I was more concerned about who I just bumped into, though. Mallory was the last person I wanted to deal with until absolutely necessary.

She played with her scarf. "I debated calling you."

"How nice."

"Archie told me about what happened to Ezra," Mallory said.

I curled my hand. Archie better not have lied to me about how he wouldn't say anything about our kiss to Mallory. More drama was the last thing I needed. Especially when my revenge plan just started.

"I can't even imagine how you must be feeling," Mallory continued.

I remained silent.

She coughed into her right arm. "Please don't be mad at Archie. I forced the truth out of him. He was growing distant, and I wanted to know what was going on. So, not like he wanted to betray your confidence."

"Great," I said.

"How are you holding up?" Mallory asked.

I suppressed my urge to cry. That could wait till I returned home. Nothing good would come from Mallory seeing me in a vulnerable state. Too much happened between us, so I couldn't be sure if she'd exploit Ezra's death in some way.

63

She shook her head. "Didn't mean to pry."

"You really don't care I've been spending time with Archie?" I asked.

"Why should I care if you're friends with Archie? I won, you lost." Mallory remained silent for a beat, biting her lip. "Sorry. Didn't mean to come across as a bitch just now. You don't deserve that as a result of everything you're going through."

"Never stopped you before."

Mallory sighed. "Okay. I deserved that."

"How was your trip out of town?" I asked.

Mallory pulled her scarf tighter. "Fine. Why do you ask?"

"Just curious."

"If you've gotta point to make, then make it. Not like I'm gonna kill you."

Goosebumps clung to my body. I couldn't laugh at Mallory being so "on the nose" with what she said. Not this time. Knowing Mallory, her comments tended to be more passive aggressive. And her venom was the last thing I needed right now. Getting emotional would only cloud the situation more.

"Life does get better," Mallory said.

"How can you possibly know that?" I asked.

She giggled, making more goosebumps spread across my arms, legs, and back—I'd just never get used to her annoying voice. "Do you have amnesia or something? Have you forgotten I've experienced loss, too?"

"I should get going."

"See you around sometime."

MONDAY, JANUARY 13

I found Archie by my front door when I opened it—I planned on going for an afternoon jog. However, the universe once again had other plans for me.

I removed the earbuds from my ears. "What are you doing here?"

Chris Bedell

"Can we talk?" He pressed his hands together. "Promise not to take up too much of your time. Please. It's important."

"Okay."

I led Archie back into my house, then locked my front door behind us. Living in a safe neighborhood didn't mean abandoning caution. Like if Mallory was nearby. There was no telling what that girl was up to. I'd even go as far as to say she was stranger than Tim Burton.

"What's on your mind?" I asked.

"It's about our conversation the other day." Archie removed his sweater, then tucked it under his armpit. He was now just wearing his white tee-shirt. For a split second, I almost gawked over him. Archie was still hot regardless of my revenge scheme. "Sorry. I was feeling kind of warm."

I raised my eyebrows. "You stopped by my house to tell me that?"

Archie laughed. "Don't be ridiculous. I just didn't wanna make you think I was gonna start stripping."

"Get to it."

"I still have feelings for you," Archie blurted.

"Where is this coming from?" I asked.

Yup. Didn't matter if there was a good chance I'd get exactly what I wanted. I still couldn't seem too eager. If I was too excited, then Archie might get suspicious. And I couldn't have that. Having as few variables as possible was the only thing that'd ensure my revenge plan went smoothly.

"I was lying to myself," he said.

I stretched my arms. "Why? You'd know I'd never wanna judge you. I'm the one who wants to witness Mallory's eternal damnation."

Archie stepped closer, so close that whatever aftershave he used tickled my skin. "Because I wanna keep kissing. In fact, I wanna do more than kissing you."

"What about Mallory?" I asked.

"She doesn't matter."

65

Between Love and Death

I continued our eye contact. "How do I know this isn't one of Mallory's crazy plans to seduce me?"

"Do you think she'd wanna share you with me after finally getting her happily ever after?" Archie asked. "Even Mallory isn't that duplicitous"

I bit my lip a little too hard and a metallic taste filled my mouth. Archie had a point, despite how I hated saying anything remotely nice about Mallory. If Mallory wanted to hurt me, then she'd be more direct.

"You really wanna be with me?" I asked.

"Yeah, but I'm tired of talking." Archie kissed me before I could respond to his comment. He dug his fingernails into my head while he shoved his tongue inside my mouth. His hands dropped to my cheeks while the kissing became more intense.

We pulled away from each other.

Archie eye-fucked me. "What do you say? Why don't we go upstairs to your bedroom, and I'll show you how much I missed you?"

I nodded, then Archie grabbed my hand and whisked me up the stairwell. I also needed to be honest with myself. The thought of hooking up with Archie was intoxicating. I was human regardless of all my current drama, and I had needs too.

I locked the bedroom door behind us, then Archie and I resumed kissing. We soon ditched our clothes, and Archie and I were on my bed before I knew it.

He intertwined his fingers with mine. "Are you sure you wanna do this?"

I looked up at Archie. "Yes."

"Good," Archie said, smiling.

"It'll be just like old times."

"Exactly."

I closed my eyes, allowing myself to be consumed by passion and lust. Sleeping with Archie wouldn't bring back Ezra, but it would move my revenge scheme along. So, at least I could have a sense of

Chris Bedell

accomplishment despite the growing emptiness in my stomach from Mom and Ezra both being dead.

BEFORE

THURSDAY, JULY 18

Wind whistled as I walked through the park in town. I somehow agreed to a meeting with Mallory, and I hoped it wouldn't be disastrous. Hanging with Mallory might not have been ideal, but I couldn't defeat her unless I knew the rules of the game. I was as clueless as ever. First with Mallory seeming genuine while visiting my mother. But then she told Archie I attacked her. The girl was batshit, and I couldn't wait to get her out of my life ASAP. Honestly, I didn't know how Kelly tolerated Mallory.

Mallory waved at me as I approached the bench. "Good to see you, Chad."

I forced a smile. "You, too."

"I have a proposition for you, and you're gonna wanna hear what I've got to say."

"That's doubtful."

She gave me a mock frown. "You could at least listen to what I've got to say before you condemn me."

I let out a breath. "Fine. What's up?"

"I'm willing to end this toxic cycle if you do one thing for me."

Chris Bedell

"I'm not sleeping with you. I'd rather poke my eyes out."

She sipped her coffee. "Ouch. I'm so hurt."

"You're wasting my time." I stood. "I've got better things to do than hang with you. My mother is dying of cancer."

Mallory played with her pigtail. "I'd never hurt your mother. You know that."

I hissed. "What do you want?"

"I want a confession from you about how you framed me for Tommy's murder."

Mallory was a lot of things, but I never considered her foolish. She couldn't have just said that. Yet blinking several times didn't change anything. I was still sitting on the park bench next to Mallory when I opened my eyes.

"How stupid do you think I am?" I asked.

"You can pat me down if you want—I'm not wearing a wire. Hell, I'll even let you check my iPhone so you can see I'm not using an app to record this conversation."

"That's okay."

Mallory scooted closer to me. "What do you say? Why don't we end this once and for all?"

Distant laughter caught my attention. A man, woman, and little boy were sitting on a blanket, having a picnic. And I couldn't help the jealousy shooting through my body. I would've given anything to have a "normal" family. I was only human, which meant I couldn't help wondering what life would've been like if Dad was still alive. Dad, Mom, and I were a cute family while it lasted.

I nibbled on the inside of my lip. Shit. This conversation wasn't the time for nostalgia. I couldn't risk crying in front of Mallory. There was a chance she could use my vulnerability against me. And I couldn't have that. Defeating Mallory was the most important thing. Even more important than needing oxygen to breathe.

"You haven't told me why you want the truth from me," I said.

69

Between Love and Death

"It'll give me closure," Mallory said.

I wrinkled my nose. "How do I know you aren't gonna keep coming for me? There's nothing to guarantee you won't change your mind about wanting revenge."

"I have other interests," she said.

I chuckled. "Such as?"

"Focusing on the colleges I wanna apply to. Kelly has also been giving me flack about staying out of trouble." Mallory rolled up her sleeves. "So, what do you say? It's just you and me here."

"I don't know," I stammered.

"I'm really not recording you."

"I believe you."

She pouted. "If you ever cared about me, then you'll do this for me."

Mallory had some nerve. There was being pushy, and then there was being manipulative. It was obvious which adjective described Mallory. If Mallory had pure intentions, then she wouldn't have badgered me into a confession.

"What about the things you've done?" I asked.

"It's no secret I got with Archie to hurt you. Everyone knows that."

I took in more deep breaths. If Mallory really wasn't recording this conversation, then there was no harm in giving her what she wanted. It wasn't like she wanted to sleep with me again. Humoring Malory could also benefit me by luring her into a false sense of security.

"Okay. You win," I said. "I framed you for Tommy's murder even though I knew Kelly was responsible."

"Do you regret what you did?" Mallory asked.

I gave her a dirty look. "This a trick question?"

"You can be honest with me. I'd never judge."

I whipped my head back and forth several times. "Nope. I don't regret doing what was necessary to protect my relationship with Archie. You've been gunning for me since when I rejected you the first day of junior year."

The bush behind us rustled before someone coughed. I tilted my head, then my heart lurched. Archie stood behind the bush.

"What are you doing here, Archie?" I asked.

Archie wove his arms together. "I can't believe you lied to me."

The air around me might as well have been spinning. My worst fear came true and nothing could change that fact. Archie knew what I did to Mallory, and I wouldn't be able to lie my way out of the situation. Not this time.

"I should go." Mallory stood. "You two have a lot to discuss."

Mallory walked away without another word, leaving Archie and me to ourselves.

I rushed towards him, but he raised his hand at me.

"We aren't having this conversation here—not now," he said. "I just can't stand the sight of you, Chad. You aren't the person I thought you were."

SATURDAY, JULY 20

I rang Archie's doorbell several times while afternoon sunlight beamed against the ground.

Archie hadn't responded to any of my texts, emails, or calls, and that wasn't okay. He was my boyfriend. We were supposed to work out our problems. I'd give him the same curtesy if the situation were reversed.

The door opened a couple of minutes later. It was Archie.

His eyes bulged. "What the hell do you want?"

"You can't just ignore me forever," I said.

Archie shut the door behind him, then scoffed. "I gave you opportunities to tell the truth, and you continued living a lie."

"Mallory isn't innocent." I wiped sweat from my forehead. "She might not have killed Tommy, but she is guilty of other things."

"And what's that?" he asked.

"Killing Jordon and Parker," I blurted.

Between Love and Death

"You're reaching."

I stepped closer. "I'm not. You can even ask Kelly if you don't believe me. She saved the newspaper articles about Jordon and Parker."

"I'm not interested in anything you have to say," Archie said.

"How can you be so cold?"

"Because you let me down."

"Newsflash, Archie. But the world isn't black and white. I did what I needed to." I grabbed his hand, but he swatted me away. "Why can't we have a redo, and forget this whole mess? What do you say?"

His nostrils flared. "We're beyond that."

"What? We're done?"

A blank expression lingered on Archie's face while a few tears dotted my eyes. Archie and I couldn't be over. There had to be something I could do. I just wasn't thinking hard enough. Yeah. A solution would arise—I just knew it.

"Gonna pretend you're perfect?" I asked.

"Never said I was."

"But you have no problem acting like a self-righteous hypocrite?" My breathing became more rapid. I lost more and more control of the conversation with each passing second. And if I wasn't careful, then my relationship would really be over.

The trees bobbed in the wind while Archie remained silent. And that was the last thing I wanted. Archie should've been trying to save this relationship.

"I love you," I pleaded.

"That's not enough," Archie said.

Archie could've ran me over with a car and it would've hurt less. Our love for each other wasn't some magic potion. But the devotion we shared to each other was a good foundation. Archie shouldn't have tossed our love aside like it didn't matter. If the situation were reversed, then Archie would beg for forgiveness.

72

Chris Bedell

"This is so unfair." I made a fist while more tears dripped down my face. Archie and I were over, and there wasn't a damn thing I could do to save the relationship. At most, I'd be lucky to have the last word. "Regardless of whether you believe me about Parker and Jordon, Mallory still manipulated the situation so you'd hear my confession. And have you forgotten Mallory lied about me giving her a black eye?"

"Mallory confessed to lying. Unlike you, she values honesty."

"We deserve better than some tragic ending."

He sucked in a breath. "Are you listening to yourself? Seems like you're desperate to hold onto me."

My heart sank. There was no reason for Archie to be cruel. Archie was my first real relationship, so I was bound to be overwhelmed by emotions from time to time. It wasn't like I stalked him 24/7 or threatened to kill myself over him. So, Archie should've been more considerate with his words. That would've been the decent thing to do.

"That's it then?" I asked.

He put his hands on his hips. "Yup. I don't wanna hear from you, see you, or talk to you in any way, shape, or form."

Archie went back inside, then slammed the door behind him.

Dread filled my insides. I didn't deserve Archie dumping me on top of Mom's terminal cancer diagnosis. So yeah, Mallory was gonna pay. That was a promise.

73

AFTER

MONDAY, JANUARY 27

I sat at a table at Café Tomorrow, enjoying my caramel latte. I decided to get out of the house and clear my head before dinner. Having various thoughts swirl through my mind couldn't be helped. Like how much longer I was gonna keep hooking up with Archie before arranging for Mallory to catch us.

Two people approached my table. It was Rebecca and Dan.

"Do you have a sec?" Rebecca asked.

"Why would I ever chat with you?" I asked.

Rebecca and Dan sat at my table and I almost screamed. I had better things to do than make superficial conversation with my former friends. I didn't owe them anything after everything that happened. I had no doubt life would be simpler if they minded their own business. It wasn't like I threatened to shoot them the night I was released from jail.

Dan gave me a weak smile. "We've been thinking a lot about you."

I drank more of my caramel latte. "Wonderful."

"You haven't returned any of our calls or texts." Rebecca gripped her ponytail. "Don't you think that's kinda rude?"

"Are you fucking kidding me?" I asked.

74

Dan gave Rebecca a look.

Rebecca sighed. "Sorry. Didn't mean for what I said to come out wrong. It'd just be nice to keep in touch."

My back ached and I sat up straighter in my chair. "Why would I ever wanna be friends with you? You abandoned me after Mallory exposed everything. Do you have any idea what it was like to be rotting in jail, awaiting trial for a crime I didn't commit?"

"You shot Mallory," Rebecca said.

"You've got no fucking idea what my life is like," I barked.

"Then tell us." Dan grabbed a napkin from the metal dispenser on the table. After that, he broke it into numerous pieces before blowing them about. Good to know I wasn't the only person who needed weird distractions to calm myself.

"We know Ezra died," Rebecca said.

Rebecca needed to shut her mouth—she had no right to mention Ezra. Rebecca wasn't my friend, and I didn't owe her any personal details about my life. Nope. Those days were long gone. And I was better off without Rebecca and Dan. They might not have sent me to jail for a murder I didn't commit, but they were no better than Mallory. Anyone with half a brain should've realized taking Mallory's side was dumb. Mallory was a troubled girl, and she didn't deserve anyone's support.

"I'm not discussing that with you," I said.

Dan sipped his tea. "You need to let your feelings out."

"Ezra has been dead for over a month," I said.

"You could've contacted us," Rebecca said.

I grunted. "You never visited me while I was in jail and you allowed yourselves to be deluded into thinking I was guilty of murder."

"Are you saying Mallory killed Kelly?" Dan asked.

"I don't know. You tell me," I said.

Rebecca scratched the top of her head. "It is odd Kelly's body was never discovered. We know how that turned out with Tommy..."

Between Love and Death

I finished my drink. "I don't wanna discuss Kelly."

"Fair enough," Dan said.

Rebecca leaned forward. "We want you to know we still plan on keeping your secret. We aren't going to snitch on you for shooting Mallory."

Please. They shouldn't have acted like they were doing me any favors. Not snitching on me was the least they could do after choosing Mallory's side over mine last summer. Real friends supported each other unconditionally. But that mantra didn't apply to Rebecca and Dan. I wasn't good enough to be their friend, and I'd have to shove aside any fleeting feelings of nostalgia. Humiliating Archie, and destroying Mallory, were the only things that mattered to me. I couldn't afford anymore hurt after all my mistreatment.

"How kind of you," I said.

"We're really trying!" Dan banged his fist against the wooden table, then glanced around us. Nobody saw his outburst. Although that might have been because there were only a couple of other customers in the shop.

"The world will survive if we aren't friends," I said.

Yeah. I didn't have one ounce of regret for my not wanting to be bothered by Rebecca and Dan. It wasn't my job to prop them up and soothe their guilty consciences. If they wanted a morality boost, then they could go elsewhere. I was the victim, not them. And Rebecca and Dan needed to stop twisting the narrative and making this about themselves. Fuck their feelings. Rebecca and Dan weren't burned with a cigarette lighter and assaulted.

Rebecca grimaced. "Please don't be so stubborn. There's no reason for you to be alone."

"I'm not. I have Gemma," I touted.

Dan snorted. "Gemma is hardly a model citizen."

The shop door opened when a woman strutted into Café Tomorrow. Wind swooshed inside, sending chills up my back while Dan's comment weighed on my mind. There was no way he said what he did. If I had a choice between saving Gemma or saving Dan and Rebecca, then I'd choose Gemma. Loyalty was one of the most important qualities in a friend, and that trait always deserved rewarding.

"She's been more supportive than you two," I said.

"Tell us how we can help," Rebecca said.

I grabbed my cup—I wasn't one of those lazy people who didn't throw out their trash. "Leave me the fuck alone!"

"We wanna be there for you," Dan said.

"Like when I was burned with a cigarette lighter and almost beaten to death?" I asked, making sure not to raise my voice. Couldn't risk people overhearing what I said. Discussing a horrific experience—such as what happened to me in prison—wasn't something that rolled off the tongue.

Rebecca and Dan remained silent.

Their speechlessness might've been a good thing, though. They'd probably say something dumb if they tried defending themselves. It wasn't like they could go back in time and undo the last few months.

"Or what about when I reached out to you after Mallory exposed me to Archie?" I asked. "Our friendship didn't seem to matter then."

Rebecca wiped a bead of sweat from her forehead. "You're right, and we're sorry."

"Little late for contrition," I said.

"We'll do anything," Dan said.

My shoulders tensed. "Just leave me the fuck alone. You two are already experts at that, so it shouldn't be a problem."

THURSDAY, JANUARY 30

Archie and I remained in his bed with the comforter wrapped around us.

Between Love and Death

My breathing hadn't returned to normal, but the knot in my stomach wasn't because of some post-sex high. I slipped Mallory a note in her mailbox yesterday that she'd find Archie cheating on her around this time, and I prayed she'd catch us.

The bedroom door opened, revealing Mallory. She screamed at us.

"What the hell is going on?" Mallory asked.

Archie sat up in bed, then his jaw sank. "What are you doing here, Mallory? Did we have a date I forgot about?"

"I was hoping it wouldn't be true," Mallory said.

Archie's eyebrows shot up. "What are you talking about?"

Mallory shrieked at us. "Didn't wanna believe you could cheat on me, but I was wrong."

"This isn't what it looks like," Archie said.

Mallory remained silent, glaring at Archie.

"How'd you even get in my house?" Archie asked.

"The maid let me in," Mallory said.

I lifted my gaze. "The sex with Archie is as fantastic as ever. We started sleeping together shortly after Ezra died."

A couple of tears fell down Mallory's cheeks. "How could you do this to me?"

"It was bigger than both of us," Archie said.

I let out a small laugh. Archie might've been compassionate about Mom and Ezra dying, but I couldn't deny he was a fuckboy. Appearing clueless about cheating was the type of thing a player would do.

Mallory put her hands on her hips. "Seriously?"

"What do you want me to say?" Archie stammered.

"That you're sorry this happened and you'll do whatever it takes to win my forgiveness," Mallory said. "It won't be easy, but we'll overcome this like we've dealt with every other challenge."

I snickered. "Give it up, bitch. You and Archie aren't some epic love story. He was only a prize to you."

Yeah. Someone needed to give Mallory a dose of reality, and I was more than happy to do that. Mallory didn't deserve a happy ending with Archie or anyone else. I'd relish her visceral humiliation. Maybe now she'd have regret for framing me for Kelly's murder.

Mallory pointed a finger at me, shouting even louder. "Shut up, asshole! Your opinion doesn't matter."

"I enjoyed every minute of sleeping with Archie," I said. "The groaning. The moaning. The passionate kissing. Sweat rolling down our faces while we caught our breaths. But you wanna know what the best part was? He was always mine. So, if you thought you'd sail off into the sunset with Archie, then you need to check yourself back into the sanitarium. Maybe the lithium will take this time."

"I'm gonna fucking kill you." Mallory ran to the bed before jumping on it. Then she started strangling me.

I wasn't the same weak kid I was when I visited Mallory at the mental hospital last April. I'd fight back this time. Mallory needed to know she couldn't push me around anymore.

I smacked my head against Mallory's, sending her flying backwards onto the floor.

I grabbed my boxers and shorts before sliding into them in a matter of seconds. After that, I snatched my tee-shirt from the middle of the bed and put it back on.

I walked over to Mallory, who remained on the floor catching her breath, then cackled. "How does it feel to lose to me yet again?"

Mallory stood before trying to slap my right cheek. I grabbed her wrist before she could strike me and I tightened my grip.

Archie gazed into Mallory's eyes. "Maybe you should go."

"No big deal." Mallory pushed my hand off her. "We're done anyway. I'm breaking up with you."

Phew. I didn't know what I would've done if Mallory decided to work on her relationship with Archie. Making my life more challenging would've been a typical thing for the universe to do. But no. Luck was

Between Love and Death

on my side today. I bet correctly that Mallory would've had too much pride to go back to a cheater. And I'd have to hope Archie felt the same way. My plan couldn't have been for nothing. I was entitled to as much revenge as I wanted after my false imprisonment, Mom's death, and Ezra's death.

Archie blinked. "What happened to what you said a couple of minutes ago?"

"I deserve better than some lame fuckboy," Mallory said.

"I'm sorry it had to be this way," Archie said.

"Whatever." Mallory turned her attention back me, piercing me with her gaze. "As for you, be glad your mother isn't alive."

"Why?" I asked.

"Because I'm not gonna stop till you're dead," Mallory said.

I winked. "What happened to our truce?"

Mallory's lips curled. "Peace is overrated."

"Fine by me," I said.

Mallory stormed out of Archie's bedroom without another word while I suppressed my laughter. My amusement could wait till I was back at Gemma's house. Appearing too eager might make Archie suspicious, and I couldn't have that. If he discovered this was my fault, then he might go back to Mallory. And him working on his relationship with Mallory would've almost been as bad as Mom and Ezra dying. Mallory was a monster, so she didn't deserve a second chance. Not even if she got on her knees and begged for forgiveness.

MONDAY, FEBRUARY 3

Archie came over to my house after school, and we currently stood in my kitchen, having coffee.

My heart thumped at a steady pace—my pulse wasn't echoing in my ears because I practiced what I was gonna say to Archie a million times.

"I'm glad you invited me over," Archie said.

80

Chris Bedell

I elevated my eyebrows. "Really?"

Archie finished his cup, put the mug in the sink, then grabbed my hands. "Getting caught was the best thing that could've happened."

I chuckled. "Since when are you an optimist?"

"I've always loved you, Chad. I might've lost sight of it, but you're the one I wanna be with—not Mallory. She's toxic."

Perfect. Time to crush Archie's heart. I couldn't have planned the situation better if I tried. Having no doubt about Archie's feelings meant he was gonna be devastated. He'd soon know what it felt like to be betrayed by the person he loved most.

"I'm dumping you," I said

Archie's mouth gaped. "What did you just say?"

I didn't even so much as wince. "I don't wanna see you anymore."

"Where is this coming from?" Archie demanded.

"You were just sex—something to pass the time."

"You don't mean this."

I gave him a toothy smile. "I really do."

Archie made a brief fist, then unclenched it. Good to know somebody cared about controlling their temper. Humiliating Archie was one thing. But I didn't know what I'd do if Archie attacked me. He was slightly taller than I, in addition to being more muscular, so he had the advantage.

"I want an explanation," Archie said.

I continued rocking my hands back and forth while contemplating what I should tell him. He still could be tempted to reconcile with Mallory if he realized I orchestrated the whole scenario. Yet I doubted Mallory would take him back. The pain in Mallory's eyes was just that palpable.

"I only started sleeping with you so I could kick your ass to the curb," I said. "You deserve to feel the pain I did when you dumped me last summer and abandoned me when I was arrested for Mallory's murder."

81

Archie shot me an inquisitive look. "We were supposed to be beyond that?"

I rolled my eyes. "Even you can't be that dumb. You didn't think I'd magically get over my resentment, did you?"

He shrugged. "I just hoped Mallory was your target, not me."

"I haven't forgotten about Mallory."

"Let me guess. You arranged for Mallory to find us?"

Give a prize to Archie. He was a lot smarter than I realized. And if I wasn't careful, then he might be a threat to me.

"Yeah, and it was so easy. Just had to slip a note in her mailbox." I paused for a second while my gaze remained locked with Archie's. "But I doubt Mallory would take you back even if she knew I planned all this."

"You're right. Apparently, it doesn't matter that she suspects you arranged everything. She doesn't wanna be with a cheater."

"Were you gonna fix things with her?" I asked.

"No, I was minding my own business when she went ballistic."

I cracked my knuckles. "You should go."

He smacked his shoulder against mine. "We could've been happy. I hope your revenge is everything you want."

Archie exited the kitchen, then the front door slammed shut several seconds later.

I could say I regretted hurting Archie's feelings. But I didn't. Not because I was a psychopath, but because I was doing what was necessary for survival. Like it or not, Archie had mistreated me like Mallory, and he needed to be thankful I didn't wanna kill him.

So yeah, I'd have no problem sleeping at night. I was one step closer to getting everything I wanted, and there wasn't a fucking thing the universe could do.

BEFORE

MONDAY, JULY 29

Wind whipped me in the face while I exited Café Tomorrow with my caramel latte. One glance at the sky revealed it'd probably rain today. A dark gray color stained the clouds. And plus, the weather app on my iPhone said there was an 80 percent chance of rain today.

I scratched an itch on the back of my neck, then my gaze shifted. Rebecca and Dan stood in front of the bakery at the end of the block.

Deep breaths. Talking to Rebecca and Dan was necessary no matter how difficult the conversation would be. They were my friends, and I needed them on my side. And not just because I hoped I'd win Archie's forgiveness. I didn't know what I'd do without my friends. Mom's terminal diagnosis lingered in the back of my mind. I'd need a support system when Mom died.

I approached Rebecca and Dan a moment later. "Hi."

Rebecca looked up at me. "What the hell do you want?"

My heart thumped louder and faster. I had a good idea about how this conversation would unfold, but I prayed I was wrong. I didn't know what I'd do if Mallory or Archie revealed to them what I did.

83

Between Love and Death

Dan's eyebrows knitted together. "You've got some nerve talking to us after what you did. And I don't know how you can live with yourself."

Shit. My worst nightmare couldn't be true. Life already sucked with having a dying Mom, losing Archie, and Mallory winning the current round of our war. It wasn't like I always wanted life to go my way. I just needed something, anything, to hold onto. I could only take so much pain before breaking.

Rebecca snorted. "Dan is right. Just go—we've got nothing to say to you."

"There are two sides to every story," I said.

Dan stepped closer, so close that the acrid stench of whatever aftershave he used prickled my skin. "You framed an innocent girl for a crime she didn't commit."

"So?" I asked.

Dan gripped his bag tighter. "It's disgusting."

I continued biting my lip. And it was a miracle I didn't draw blood. Anyone would've realized I had a problem. On the one hand, I had the perfect response to Dan's comment. Mallory might not have killed Tommy, but she killed Parker and Jordon. But I didn't have any proof. So, flinging more accusations might make me seem like the crazy one. And that wasn't something that could happen if I wanted to regain my friendship with Dan and Rebecca.

I huffed. "Everyone makes mistakes."

Rebecca crossed her arms. "This isn't telling a lie to spare someone's feelings or saying you got almost a C on a test instead of saying you got a 69. This is someone's life, and you aren't the person we thought you were."

"Must be nice to be perfect," I said.

Dan shook his head. "We never claimed to be perfect."

"Mallory isn't a good person," I stammered. "Have you forgotten how she only became interested in Archie because I rejected her?"

84

Chris Bedell

"Her error in judgment didn't threaten your safety," Dan said.

"Imagine if Mallory was tried as an adult and went to prison," Rebecca said.

My gaze narrowed. "But she wasn't—Mallory was sent to a sanitarium. So, her safety was never in danger."

"You had no way of knowing what would happen," Dan said.

My surroundings might as well have been spinning despite how this was real life and not some whacky cartoon. I didn't see how I could regain control of this conversation. Nothing I said worked. Rebecca and Dan seemed intent on hating me, and there was a real possibility that I lost their friendship for good.

"What? That's it?" I demanded.

Dan didn't even wince. "Yup."

Wait. Not telling Dan and Rebecca about Mallory killing Jordon and Parker was one thing. But I could still tell them about Mallory's other sinister behavior. I hadn't forgotten how she followed me to Tommy's vacation home and then snuck into my bedroom one evening in hopes of confronting me. That information definitely proved Mallory was unhinged.

Rebecca and Dan started walking away from me.

"There's something you don't know!" I exclaimed.

Rebecca and Dan stopped before looking back at me.

"And what's that?" Rebecca asked.

"Mallory stalked me," I revealed. "She followed me to Tommy's vacation house and snuck into my bedroom one evening. It's only natural that I'd do whatever it takes to get that wretched girl out of my life."

Dan snickered. "You couldn't be more wrong. Mallory must've trailed you because she was scared you were probably gonna set her up for a murder she didn't commit."

Disbelief pulsed through my body. Dan couldn't have excused Mallory's antics. That was bullshit. Normal people didn't follow people

85

Between Love and Death

around for no reason. Mallory would always be creepy. It must've been engrained in her DNA.

"We're done," Dan said.

Dan and Rebecca shuffled down the block in the opposite direction and were out of sight in a matter of seconds. Rain pattered against the ground and I made a fist. Stealing my boyfriend was bad enough, but taking my only two friends from me was inexcusable. I was now more determined to destroy Mallory. I had nothing left, and I didn't know what I'd do.

TUESDAY, JULY 30

I was about to ring the doorbell while morning sunlight poked through the partially cloudy sky and nearby birds chirped when Kelly opened the door.

She gave me a funny look. "What are you doing here?"

"We need to talk," I said.

"This isn't a good time."

A lump lingered in my throat. Kelly might've been a lot things, but she hadn't lied. Not yet. She sported a tracksuit, sneakers, and she held an iPhone with earbuds plugged into it. She must've been going for a run or something.

I pressed my hands together. "This is important."

"Fine. You have five minutes."

I forced a smile. "Mallory isn't around, is she?"

"No, she's with Archie."

"Good."

Her scowl intensified. "What do you want?"

"You have to help me."

She giggled. "That's a good one. Anyone ever tell you that you'd make a great comedian?"

"This isn't a game, Kelly."

86

Chris Bedell

"There's nothing left to discuss."

"Mallory must've told you how she exposed what I did," I said.

She pushed a lock of hair to the side. "You've only got yourself to blame."

"I need you to help me win Archie back. You're the best person to prove how toxic Mallory is."

Kelly grimaced. "Doesn't matter if you've got a point. You lost any sympathy you had when you went to the sanitarium and gloated to Mallory. So, you've only got yourself to blame for your fucked up life."

I dug my nails into my palms. I hated admitting Kelly was right, but she was. If there was something I regretted other than letting Mallory in my life for too long, it was going to the mental hospital. That visit wasn't smart. That interaction with Mallory gave her all the ammunition she needed to fight back against me.

"I can't change the past," I said.

"No shit."

"You don't have to be a bitch. My mother is dying of cancer, in case that slipped your mind."

She rolled her eyes. "You aren't the only one suffering. Mallory is hanging Tommy's murder over me. And now Archie, Rebecca, and Dan also know what I did."

"It's not like she has forensic evidence," I said.

Kelly gritted her teeth. "That's not the point."

"I could've been happy with Archie."

"Sorry. Don't know what you want me to say."

Tears pricked my eyes. It shouldn't have been this hard for one thing in my life to go well. Kelly was also an adult, so she should've crafted a better response than playing the "I don't know" card. Her response was as empty as the hollow feeling inside me. I deserved to have at least one person on my side. Kelly and I were kindred spirits in a way. Being co-conspirators against Mallory was fun while it lasted. Kelly was the one

87

Between Love and Death

person who understood what having visceral hatred for Mallory entailed.

"There's a simple solution," I said.

Her eyebrows inched upward. "And what's that?"

I didn't hesitate. "Kill Mallory."

Kelly's eyes bulged. "You can't be serious?"

"Our lives would be simpler without her."

"In the spirit of being generous, I'm gonna pretend I didn't hear you."

"She turned Rebecca and Dan against me, too, and I've got nobody left."

Kelly looped her arms around me, then stared me down. "I'm sorry about what you're going through with your mother—nobody deserves that. But you've got to move on from Archie and this toxic feud with Mallory. You've got your whole life ahead of you, and you shouldn't waste your energy on Mallory."

"Life wasn't supposed to be like this," I whimpered.

Kelly released me. "It'll get better."

"Doubtful."

"I'm not a monster."

"And what the fuck is that supposed to mean?" I spat, cheeks burning. This just wasn't my week or month. I didn't know what I'd do if life didn't improve.

"I'd never willingly let Mallory commit another crime. So, if I've got reason to suspect Mallory is planning something against you, then I'll tell you."

"Whatever. You're just a stupid bitch like your sister." I pointed my right index finger at Kelly. "You were a co-conspirator in this war against Mallory, and yet I'm the only one paying for my actions. If you ask me, that's fucking bullshit."

"Sorry," she mumbled.

I shrieked at her. "Stop apologizing! I don't want you to be sorry. I just need your help in winning Archie back and destroying Mallory!"

Kelly didn't speak. Instead, she glared at me. Almost as if she wanted me gone. And that was lazy. If she wanted me to leave, then she should've said so. Being a coward was no way to go through life.

"You know what?" I bellowed. "I'm not the only one Mallory could be plotting against. Maybe Mallory wants to kill you first. But it'll be hard to do anything against Mallory when you're dead."

"Is that a threat?" she asked.

"Just stating a fact."

"Go!" Kelly screamed.

"Gladly." I stormed down the front steps without another word.

So much for wanting Kelly to help me. That conversation couldn't have gone worse if I tried. I was gonna have to figure out a way to regain my life. Mallory might've delivered a few setbacks, but I wouldn't let her win. I couldn't. My anger in this toxic feud against Mallory was the only thing I had left.

THURSDAY, AUGUST 1

I trekked down Main Street, only to scoff.

Mallory and Archie were seated at table a few feet away from me. Their gaze remained on their menus, but I wasn't gonna let them not noticing me stop me from saying something. My initial rage hadn't stopped flaring through my body because the idea of Mallory and Archie on a date was beyond nauseating.

I marched over to them. "What do we have here?"

Archie lifted his gaze off the menu. "Chad…"

Mallory twirled a strand of hair around her finger. "You should go. Wouldn't wanna make a scene."

"Spare me the fake concern," I said.

Archie coughed into his arm. "What do you want, man?"

Between Love and Death

Ouch. If I wanted further confirmation about my estrangement from Archie, then I got. Calling me "man" was the last thing I wanted. I wasn't one of Archie's bros; I was the person he was supposed to be in love with. If I wanted to act deranged, then I would've screamed at Archie.

But no.

Appearing crazy in front of Archie would give Mallory what she wanted. And I couldn't have that if I wanted to crush her. I also couldn't risk further alienating myself from Archie. If I did, then we might've been done for good.

"I'm not giving up," I said.

"Not sure what that's supposed to mean." Mallory sipped her ice water. "But give it your best shot. You've got no leverage on us."

I shifted my attention to Archie. "You seriously wanna date Mallory?"

Archie shrugged. "She makes me happy."

"You're just punishing me," I said.

Archie snickered. "If I wanted to hurt you, then I'd spit in your face."

"What a fucking joke," I said.

Mallory gestured alone. "Go! You aren't wanted here!"

I sucked on my teeth. "You're really gonna pretend Mallory wasn't interested in you to hurt me? Fuck. She's probably still pursuing you because of that."

"Nobody's perfect," Archie said.

I leaned towards Mallory, lips brushing up against her right ear. Then I whispered, "You might not have killed Tommy, but I haven't forgotten how you killed Parker and Jordon. So, enjoy this victory while you can."

I darted away from Archie and Mallory. The odds might've been against me, but I wouldn't let anyone get me down forever. Mallory must've had a weakness, and I'd find it. Even if it was the last thing I did. That was a promise.

AFTER

MONDAY, FEBRUARY 17

I sat at a table in back of Café Tomorrow, enjoying my caramel latte.

Getting out of the house was best. I could only spend so much time each day in the home Mom died in. No offense to Mom, but home sort of resembled a haunted house. It was strange to think of my house as the place Mom once *lived* as opposed to *was living at*. So yeah, I'd never shake Mom's death. The event lingered in every little thing that happened to me.

Someone tapped my back.

"Hi," said a guy.

I looked up at the person.

Shit. Archie stood in front of me and I wanted to kick myself. I shouldn't have stopped at Café Tomorrow. Gemma mentioned something about today being a professional development day for teachers, so students had the day off. And I should've anticipated how the universe would fuck with me, and that I'd run into Archie, Mallory, or Rebecca and Dan.

"What do you want?" I asked.

He beamed his eyes. "Can we talk?"

91

Between Love and Death

I didn't respond. Archie must've taken my silence as approval since he sat in the chair next to me.

"Not trying to upset you or anything." Archie paused for a beat. "We just need to chat about a couple of things."

"We've got nothing to discuss. I repeatedly slept with you so I could dump you."

"I don't believe you."

"Doesn't matter. It's the truth."

He leaned closer. "You must have a lot of anger—especially about your mother. And I don't blame you. I'd be devastated, too."

I hissed. "I didn't even get to say goodbye to my mother before she died. Do you understand that, Archie?"

Archie's jaw quaked. "Sorry."

"Leave me alone."

"Things might be difficult between us, but we can fix our relationship. We just need to put in some effort."

I would've laughed if I hadn't just sipped more of my beverage. Archie must've misspoken. He couldn't have wanted to hold onto our relationship. But I wasn't having a dream or hallucinating. This conversation was as a real as anything else.

I'd have to do something about my confusion, though. Archie's concern for our relationship was misplaced. It shouldn't have taken dire circumstances for him to actually care. I'd never be one of those people who prided themselves in morality. I couldn't. Life was complicated, and there was such a thing as toxic positivity. I couldn't live on sunshine and smiles forever. The world was a cruel place. And the sooner people realized it, the better off they'd be.

"How desperate are you?" I asked.

"Come again?"

"You're hanging onto this relationship like it's a life jacket. Perhaps you only want me because I'm no longer interested in you."

92

Chris Bedell

He wrinkled his nose. "That's not true, and you know it. I wouldn't have slept with you all those times if our connection wasn't real."

"What I had with Ezra was real. You were only a means to an end."

He pouted. "What do you want me to do?"

"Leave me the fuck alone. Walking away is what you do best."

"Alienating the one person you have left isn't smart."

"I've got Gemma."

"You should keep better company than her."

I glared at Archie. "Where was the concern when I was arrested for a murder I didn't commit? Could've used support then."

"I can't change the past."

"Excuses. Excuses."

"I'm really trying," Archie said.

"My mother's birthday is later in the week, so I don't need your bullshit."

He clapped his hand over his mouth. "Sorry. I had no idea."

"Don't worry about it. You aren't my boyfriend, so you don't owe me anything. Understand?"

He chuckled. "Won't being with me make Mallory jealous? I mean, isn't that your ultimate goal?"

"That's a beginning, not an ending." I finished the rest of my caramel latte. But the sweetness from the caramel stuck at the bottom of the mug escaped me. Normally, I would've savored the last couple of drops of caramel. But not today. Archie was the last thing I needed. My pulse hummed louder in my ears. This conversation seemed no closer to finishing. And I might've even had myself to blame. Archie didn't have a gun pointed at me, so I could leave whenever I wanted. Yet, I didn't flee. Almost as if I wanted Archie to feel the contempt I had for him— the same visceral anger I had for Mallory.

Archie reached for my hand with his, but I squatted at it. "I'd love to visit your mother's grave with you. Maybe we could bring your mom's favorite flowers."

93

Between Love and Death

"Nice idea. Write it down so you can use it in a poem."

He glanced at my empty mug, then resumed eye contact. "Want me to get you a refill?"

"If you've got something to say, then you should say it."

Archie put his arms on the table, then slid them forward. "Only trying to make a joke."

"I do have one question," I said.

He winked. "And what's that?"

I snickered. "How does it feel?"

"You're gonna have to be more specific."

"I'm talking about being used. You must feel humiliated that you were gullible enough to allow yourself to be played."

Yeah. If Archie insisted on prolonging this conversation, then I'd make a jab ... or ten. I wasn't the same kid I was when the cops handcuffed and shoved me into the police car last August. I'd rather be feared than loved, because love got me nothing—whether it was platonic or romantic. My relationship with Archie was long gone. Mom was dead. And Archie was dead. So, my anger was the only thing I had left. I wouldn't let anyone steal that from me, like everything else that had been taken from me.

He shook his head. "Nice try, but that isn't gonna work."

"I've got no idea what you're talking about."

"You can insult me all you want, but you're never gonna push me away." Archie sighed. "We're meant for each other, and you'll realize that one day. Maybe not right away. But you will eventually, and I hope for your sake I'm still single when you realize that."

My gaze narrowed. "Enjoying being a fuckboy?"

"Kinda harsh."

"Not if my comment is true," I spat.

Archie played with the ends of his scarf, and my spine tingled—I would've recognized that scarf anywhere. I got it for him last winter

94

Chris Bedell

when we were dating. Shit. I'd never accept how one year ago felt like another lifetime.

"I'm willing to do whatever it takes to get our relationship back on track," Archie said.

"Can you bring back my mother? Can you bring back Ezra?" I demanded.

"No," he mumbled.

I stood and didn't push my chair in. "That's what I thought."

"Wait!" Archie exclaimed.

"What?"

Archie pulled my arm. "We aren't done."

"Damn you." I returned to my seat, then gave Archie a dirty look. "What more do we have to discuss? We've already established I hate you."

"Doesn't have to be this way," Archie said.

"Too much has happened for our relationship to be salvageable."

Archie loosened his collar. "I don't believe that. Not for a second."

Archie was beyond pathetic. He should've taken my hint much earlier in the conversation. Nothing he said mattered. We'd never have a real relationship, and he needed to move on with his life. He was only setting himself up for disappointment by continuing to hold onto a future that'd never exist.

"It's the truth," I said.

"There's one thing I want from you."

"My patience is long gone," I said.

The door opened and wind swished inside Café Tomorrow while a woman entered. My teeth chattered, and I rubbed my hands together, creating friction. Another reminder of how it was still winter. I would've given anything for it to be spring. Nothing like new beginnings to make you feel good.

"What are your plans for Mallory? You can't seriously wanna kill her?" he asked.

95

Between Love and Death

"Don't ask questions you don't want the answers to."

THURSDAY, FEBRUARY, 20

I left the local grocery store around four in the afternoon, only to bump into Rebecca and Dan. Rebecca halted her shopping cart and frowned.

Great. A judgmental lecture was the last thing I needed on Mom's birthday. Life was already cruel enough, and I didn't need the morality police after me.

"Chad," Dan mumbled.

I gripped my plastic grocery bag harder. "I've gotta go."

"What are you doing here?" Dan asked.

"Today is my mother's birthday, so I wanted to buy Tiramisu. That was her favorite type of cake," I said.

Rebecca pursed her lips. "We know what you did to Archie, and you should be ashamed of yourself. What kind of person sleeps with someone so they can arrange for both their girlfriend to catch them and then dump them?"

"Archie deserved it," I blurted.

My throat burned. I mentioned today was Mom's birthday, and Rebecca and Dad hadn't said shit. Some friends they were. If they cared about me, then they would've dropped this lecture and treated me like a human. No matter how awful they thought I was, I was still the boy who lost his mother to cancer at seventeen. No well-coined phrase would ever encompass the emotional violence I experienced from losing my mom so early in life. This was real life, not a daydream. I'd just have to live with the pain like I always did.

Rebecca stuffed her hands into her coat pockets. "You used to be such a different person, Chad. What happened to you?"

"Mallory happened. Archie happened. My mother died. Ezra died." I grunted at them. "So, have your pick about why I'm so fucked up."

Dan exhaled a breath. "Life doesn't have to be this way. You don't have to hold onto the anger anymore. It'll consume you."

I cackled. "Thanks, dad."

A woman—who was accompanied by two children—pushed her shopping cart by us and entered the grocery store. I might not have known anything about her or the two children, but I wouldn't have minded trading places with them. Switching lives would've been better than feeling trapped by my agony. The agony I felt from how too much had happened for Archie and I to reunite. The agony I felt from everything Mallory did to me. The agony I felt from lying in bed, contemplating what I did to deserve having Mom die of cancer when I should've been sleeping. The agony I felt from knowing Ezra and I would never have a future together.

Nearby trees shook after more wind roared, sending clumps of ice and snow onto the ground. Damn. Spring needed to arrive ASAP. I didn't know how many more ways I could say it–I was tired of winter.

My nostrils flared. "Here's an idea. Why don't you stay out of my way, and I'll stay out of your way?"

I didn't wait for a response. Instead, I hurried to my car. Not engaging with someone was sometimes best. Nothing good would come from hashing out the same argument with Rebecca and Dan. They knew why I acted the way I did, and if they couldn't accept me, then that was their problem. I didn't need their approval because I didn't need my actions to be validated by anyone else. I could live with the person I was, and that was the only thing that mattered.

BEFORE

THURSDAY, AUGUST 15

I exited a boutique on Main Street, carrying several bags of clothes. Mom gave me her credit card to buy some back-to-school clothes. The only condition was I couldn't spend more than $120.

I took several deep breaths. Mallory was approaching me and I didn't know what to do. I could either make superficial small talk with her or we could have toxic banter. I'd choose the later, though. I might've been a lot of things, but Mallory needed to know what she did wasn't okay. She couldn't steal my life—my relationship with Archie and friendship with Rebecca and Dan—and think she'd get away with her deception. Mom was the only person she hadn't stolen from me, and it needed to stay that way. I refused to let Mallory dictate the fleeting amount of time Mom had left. There also wasn't anybody around as the street was empty except for us. So, no harm in having it out. Standing up for myself was something I'd never apologize for. I couldn't.

"Stalking me?" I asked.

Mallory giggled. "You wish."

"This little game between us isn't over."

Chris Bedell

"What are you gonna do?" Mallory adjusted her purse strap, pulling it up her arm more. "Have another chat with Kelly?"

My jaw lowered. I didn't know how Mallory knew about my previous conversation with her sister. Kelly didn't seem stupid enough to tell Mallory about our heated exchange. If Kelly wasn't careful, then Mallory might send Kelly right to jail. But somehow Mallory was privy to what happened a couple of weeks ago. Almost as if Mallory returned to stalking me.

Mallory snorted. "Relax. Kelly didn't snitch on your conversation. I know about your meeting with Kelly because I arrived home earlier from running errands and saw you leaving the front porch in a huff."

Creepy. It didn't matter how much time passed since we were genuine friends. Apparently, Mallory would always have some intuitive vibe about the thoughts swirling in my mind. And I didn't know what I was gonna do. Knowing my every thought and move could be dangerous. When I ended her for good, Mallory couldn't know it was coming. Surprise was the one advantage I could have, and I couldn't mess it up. Not if I wanted to decimate Mallory.

I placed my hands on my hips. "Yet I didn't see you."

"I'm like a ninja."

I laughed. "You wish."

"I'd be careful if I were you, Chad."

I shot her a look. "And why is that? You already took my boyfriend and best friends from me. It's not like you can do any worse."

"That a challenge?" Mallory asked.

I should've fretted in response to Mallory's comment. But I didn't. I was used to her antics by now. The once sweet, innocent girl was long gone. And my continued thought about how the feud between us wouldn't end until one of us was dead remained true. The world wasn't big enough to handle both of us. So, one of us would be dead by the end of senior year. That was a promise. This conflict couldn't go on forever.

Between Love and Death

I also had better things to do with the rest of my life than be consumed by this petty game till I was in my eighties.

"Archie belongs with me," I said.

"He's over you—your relationship was a phase."

"Do you even care about him?" I demanded.

She batted her eyes. "What do you think?"

"Arrogance is a dangerous thing."

"I could say the same about you."

"I'm not cocky," I said.

She grabbed a hair tie from her pocket, ran her fingers through her hair, then put her hair in a ponytail. "You were dumb enough to walk into my trap and have Archie discover what you did."

"You might have a point there..."

"Face it. I'm smarter than you," Mallory said.

"In your dreams."

Mallory licked her lips. "Tell me something. How's your mother doing these days? I hope time isn't moving too quickly. I'd hate for your last few months with your mother to be rushed."

Mallory needed to be careful about the next thing that came out of her mouth. Mom already had enough to deal with, and didn't need someone as evil as Mallory bothering her.

I curled my fingers into a fist. "You better not be threatening my mother. If you do anything to her, then I'll kill you. Fuck. I'd kill you for free."

"Your temper is gonna get you into trouble," she said.

"My anger is justified."

She gave me a mock frown. "Never said it wasn't. Just that you need to be careful. Life has a funny way of changing on a moment's notice."

"That a threat?" I asked.

She extended her arms, then straightened my shirt collar. Goosebumps formed on my back, arms, and legs. Nothing comforting

Chris Bedell

existed from Mallory's touch. If anything, I wished I was a snake and could shed my skin. No telling where Mallory's hands might've been.

"Enjoy the next few days while you can," Mallory said.

I raised my brow. "What are you up to?"

"Nothing," she said.

"Why don't I believe you?"

"Paranoia isn't a good look. You might wanna go to a doctor and seek help." Mallory patted my shoulder before strutting away in the opposite direction.

My stomach did cartwheels. Mallory's antics might not be new, but I would've been lying if I didn't acknowledge the trepidation shooting through my body. If Mallory was capable of driving a wedge between me and the various people in my life, then there was no telling what else she had planned.

TUESDAY, AUGUST 20

Mom and I sat on stools in front of the kitchen counter. Her eyes remained glued to the local newspaper. But she needed to stop reading the headline. Murder wasn't healthy to dwell on. Especially when it was an unexpected death.

"I can't believe Kelly is dead." Mom pushed the newspaper to the side. "This town is something else. First Tommy and now Kelly."

A lump lingered in my throat. "Yeah, it's sad."

Mom eyed me. "You didn't have anything to do with Kelly's death, did you?"

"Where would I hide her body?" I asked.

Mom stroked her right cheek, then finished her coffee. "Don't remind me. The thought of someone being declared dead without an actual body is kind of twisted. Then, the loved ones will be left wondering if there's a small possibility the person is alive. And don't even get me started on the crime scene. Can you imagine how much

Between Love and Death

blood there must've been for the detectives to say the amount of blood loss meant Kelly had to be dead?"

"Unless they wanted the person dead."

"Are you implying Mallory killed Kelly?" Mom grabbed a Kleenex, blew her nose, then tossed the tissue into the garbage under the sink.

"You said it, not me."

Mom shuddered. "Mallory might not be the most ethical person, but murder is extreme."

"Nothing surprises me these days."

The doorbell rang.

"I'll see who's at the door." I left the kitchen to open the front door.

My heart almost jumped into my throat from the sight of the men that stood on my front porch. It was Detective Bonnie Jones and Detective Garrison—the detectives who questioned me during the investigation of Tommy's murder.

Detective Jones grinned. "May we come in?"

"I suppose I don't have a choice?" I asked.

Detective Garrison grunted. "Not really."

Detective Jones elbowed her partner. "What Skip is trying to say is that we'd appreciate your cooperation. Although we have a warrant."

The word lingered in my mind for a beat. Warrant. No. No. No. I couldn't have been under arrest.

I let out the loudest scream of my life. "Mom!"

Footsteps echoed, and Mom soon appeared by my side.

Mom placed a hand on my shoulder. "What's going on, sweetie?"

"These detectives mentioned something about a warrant," I said.

A gust of wind howled, slamming the front door shut. Oops. Must've forgotten to close the door in all the excitement of being visited by the detectives.

"You can't just come into my house like you own it," Mom said.

Detective Jones chewed on the inside of her lip. "Let's start with the questions first."

102

Chris Bedell

"Okay," I said.

"Where were you between 9 and 10 AM last Friday?" Detective Garrison asked.

I lifted my brow. "Are you implying I killed Kelly?"

Yeah. I asked my question regardless of my increased pulse. I needed to know the rules of the game if I was gonna win. And I'd just have to hope Mallory wasn't behind this. Killing her own sister and then framing me would've been a new low. At least I hadn't murdered anyone when I set her up for Tommy's murder.

"This would go smoother if you would just answered the question," Detective Jones said.

"I went for a jog a couple of minutes after nine," I said. "Usually takes me an hour and then I jump in the shower when I get home."

Detective Jones looked at Mom. "Can you alibi him?"

"No, I left at eight for a spa day with friends," Mom said.

"You can't arrest me for Kelly's murder without probable cause," I said, raising my voice. "This isn't a dictatorship."

"But we do have a warrant," Detective Garrison retorted.

"For what?" I spat.

Detective Jones coughed into her left arm. "For a DNA sample. More specifically, a mouth swab."

"What about Mallory?" I asked. "Check that shit out."

Mom squeezed my shoulder.

"Kelly has been nothing but supportive since Mallory was released from the sanitarium in June," Detective Garrison said.

"Let's just get this over with," Detective Jones said.

I heaved out a sigh. "Fine. But it doesn't mean I'm gonna enjoy this."

"I'm sure the DNA sample will clear everything up," Detective Jones said. "A nice boy such as yourself doesn't fit the profile of a killer."

How kind of Detective Jones to defuse the situation. That was more than could be said for her loser partner who hadn't stopped scowling at me since he entered my house. Being dedicated to his job was one thing.

Between Love and Death

But not if it meant pursuing a witch hunt against an innocent person. Last time I checked, I was innocent till proven guilty.

I rolled my eyes. "Just do it already!"

"That's the spirit!" Detective Jones exclaimed.

The universe was on my side—for the moment, at least. Detective Jones took the mouth swab, not her partner. The detectives left after obtaining the DNA sample. And them leaving was for the best. If I was gonna go down for Kelly's murder, then I didn't feel like spending my last few days or hours arguing.

"We've got a big problem," Mom finally said.

I gave Mom a look. "What's up? You don't believe I killed Kelly, do you?"

"You aren't the issue."

"Then what is it?"

Mom averted her gaze. "Mallory stopped by a couple of days before Kelly died—she wanted to give me cookies."

"Did you get acute mercury poisoning or something?"

"The cookies aren't the issue," Mom snapped, face growing redder.

Damn. I didn't like the sound of where Mom's story was headed. If Mallory hadn't poisoned the cookies, then I couldn't imagine what else would be so bad that Mom hadn't stopped shaking.

"She asked to use the bathroom," Mom said. "What if she stole hair from your comb or brush, and planted it at the scene of the crime in her living room?"

"You don't think Mallory would do that, do you?"

"She took a long time in the bathroom."

I rocked my hands back and forth. "Fuck. I'm gonna go to jail for a murder I didn't commit, aren't I?"

Mom hugged me. "I'm so sorry, honey. I never thought Mallory would do something so evil."

"It's not your fault."

104

Yeah. I wouldn't waste time being angry with Mom. She'd never intentionally try to hurt me, unlike Mallory. Mom had nothing to gain by my pain—whether emotional or physical. She wasn't a psychopath like Mallory.

"If Mallory is behind this, then she won't get away with this," Mom said.

My breathing slowed for a sec. It didn't matter if what Mom said was true. She comforted me, and that was what I needed. It wasn't like the police were gonna arrest me this second. So, yeah. I still had some time left.

"Thanks," I mumbled.

THURSDAY, AUGUST 22

I opened the front door only to be greeted by Detective Jones and Detective Garrison. I didn't need to be a genius to realize that they must not have had good news. The blank expressions on their faces revealed everything worth knowing.

I forced a laugh. "What can I do for you?"

"We wish we had better news, but the DNA sample came back as a positive match for the hairs found at the crime scene," Detective Jones said.

I scratched the side of my head. Fuck. Mom must've been right. Perhaps Mallory went to the bathroom so she could collect my DNA and plant it in her living room. I cocked my head. The sunlight beaming from the sky glinted against the object in Detective Garrison's hands. More specifically, handcuffs.

Fuck. My fate was sealed, and I should've taken Mallory's previous cryptic threat more seriously.

Detective Jones flinched after taking a deep breath—good to know she had a small conscience. "You're under arrest for Kelly's murder. You have the right to remain silent. Anything you say can and will be

Between Love and Death

used against you in a court of law. You have the right to an attorney. If you cannot afford an attorney, one will be provided to you."

I nodded.

Detective Garrison handcuffed me, then I screamed louder than I did the other day. The front door burst open, revealing Mom.

"What's going on?" Mom asked.

"Your son is under arrest," Detective Garrison said.

"Based on one DNA sample?" Mom asked. "Do you know how many times Chad has been to Mallory and Kelly's home? I'm sure it's normal for a couple of his hairs to be there."

"We would agree with you. But there's more," Detective Jones said.

My gaze remained on the ground. "The fuck you talking about?"

"We have Kelly's diary," Detective Jones revealed. "More specifically, entries revealing your growing hostile relationship. How you were becoming jealous and obsessed with Mallory. And how you kept seeking Kelly out so you could turn her against Mallory."

Mom sobbed. "You can't arrest someone because of diary entries."

"We checked the handwriting with a sample," Detective Garrison said. "The handwriting matches Kelly's."

Mom wailed louder. Not that I blamed her or anything. I'd be a wreck, too, if I were in her position. I couldn't imagine the various emotions weighing on her mind. Having her only child arrested for murder was one hell of way to end the summer.

"Where are you taking him?" Mom asked.

"County jail," Detective Garrison said.

"You can't do that. He's just a baby," Mom said.

"Chad's eighteen, so he's technically an adult," Detective Garrison replied.

Yeah. My birthday was a few days ago. And I hadn't dwelled on it because this just wasn't my year. It wasn't like I had anything to be happy or thankful for.

"This is bullshit," Mom said.

106

Chris Bedell

"We're done." Detective Garrison grabbed me, then pushed me down the steps. Almost as if he wanted to herd me like cattle. Like I was less than human.

I arrived at my driveway and was shoved into the backseat of the police car in a matter of seconds before the detectives hopped into the front seats. Detective Garrison barreled out of my driveway, and my house was soon no longer visible.

I arrived in the room where they took mugshots sometime later, and Detective Garrison took the photos.

He led me out of the room after he finished taking the photos. The uneasiness returned to my stomach from his vigorous pushing. Like I was once again a piece of cattle being led to my slaughter.

We arrived at an empty cell a couple of minutes later and the guard opened it. Detective Garrison shoved me inside, then snickered once he was out of the cell.

"Enjoy your stay," Detective Garrison said.

The guard locked the cell and the clanking echoed.

Fuck. Mallory had me where she wanted me. I was all alone and there wasn't a fucking thing I could do about it. For the moment, at least.

107

AFTER

MONDAY, MARCH 2

Grey clouds veiled the sky while I exited Café Tomorrow with my caramel latte. And unfortunately for me, the universe was in the mood to stick it to me. Archie was fast approaching me and there wasn't a fucking thing I could do about it. Letting Archie say whatever it was that he wanted to say was easier than pretending I didn't see him and walking on the opposite side of the street. Archie knew where I lived, after all. So, if Archie really wanted to chat with me, then I had no doubt that he'd find a way.

Archie gave me a small smile. "Fancy seeing you here."

I wrinkled my nose. "Were you following me or something?"

"Don't flatter yourself. I just felt like getting a cup of coffee from the best place in town."

I rolled my eyes. "Way to lay it on thick."

"You know I'm right. Why else would you keep going to Café Tomorrow?"

"Just say what you came to say, so I can continue on with my day."

"Pushing me away won't work forever."

"Excuse me?"

108

He smirked. "I'm serious, Chad. I mean, you might've convinced yourself that you don't feel anything for me. But you and I both know that isn't true."

"Learn to take no for an answer."

"We were great together, and we still could be."

I snickered. "Even you aren't that stupid. I was just your backup."

Archie tucked his hands into his jacket pockets. "That's not true, and you know it. Have you forgotten who I met first?"

"You seemed to enjoy your time with Mallory."

His face drooped. "What I had with Mallory wasn't real. Besides, she never understood me the way you did."

"You just don't wanna be alone."

"What's the game plan?" Archie asked. "I mean, what are you gonna do once your revenge is all over?"

Archie might not have winced, twitched, or frowned during this conversation, but he couldn't fool me. Not entirely, at least. Archie had to have been a little nervous. He just said "I mean" for the second time. And I didn't need a degree in linguistics to know a more confident person would have gotten more to the point when speaking.

I let out a loud laugh. "My life is none of your business."

"It is if I become collateral damage in your war with Mallory."

"You don't have to worry about that."

Archie winked. "And why's that?"

I snorted. "Did you forget the part where I dumped you after arranging for Mallory to catch us in bed? Perhaps you need help with your memory."

"You can't seriously think you'll get away with killing Mallory?"

"I won't know until I try." I paused for a moment. "Imagine how differently life would've been if Mallory never decided to pursue you at the beginning of junior year."

"We can't change the past."

"You're absolutely right. But that doesn't mean I can't win the war."

Between Love and Death

Archie furrowed his eyebrows. "It's all a game to you?"

"Forget it. You just don't understand."

Archie stepped closer—so close that the acrid stench of whatever aftershave he used wafted through the air and stung my nostrils. "You were hoping to have a happily ever after with Ezra once you defeated Mallory, right?" he asked.

Out of all the things Archie could've mentioned, Ezra was the last thing I expected to come up when chatting with him. It wasn't like Archie ever met Ezra.

I nodded. "Yes, I was gonna help Ezra once I sorted out the Mallory situation. Not everyone is guilty for what they've been accused of."

"What the fuck does that mean?"

"The person who accused Ezra of beating him lied because he hates him." I averted my gaze. "Only now Ezra can't get justice."

"It's not your fault that Ezra died."

"Maybe. Maybe not," I finally said.

No offense to Archie, but he didn't need to state the obvious. Anyone with even a little common sense could infer it wasn't my fault that Ezra died. No, that honor belonged to whoever stabbed Ezra in the shower.

An icy sensation washed over me while Ezra lingered in my mind. Imagining what his last few moments of life were like was the last thing I wanted to contemplate. Yet here I was, praying his final moments were at least quick if they weren't painless.

My stomach churned. Ezra was yet another example of how the world was a messed-up place. Someone as awful as Mallory being able to roam free while Ezra died didn't sit well with me. Mallory deserved a thousand deaths.

"I'm still willing to give things a second chance with us despite everything that you've done."

"I'm good."

"One day you'll get lonely."

"I don't need you to tell me how the rest of my life is gonna unfold."

Chris Bedell

His eyes widened. "So, what? You're gonna mooch off of Gemma for the rest of her life?"

"It was her choice to give me half of her money," I snapped, cheeks burning.

"Money can't buy happiness."

Annoyance bubbled inside me. People touting the expression about money not buying happiness were beyond delusional. Like it or not, the world revolved around money. If someone wanted to attend college, that cost money. If someone wanted to do a home improvement project, that cost money. If someone wanted to take a vacation, that cost money. And so on, and so on.

"Let's agree to disagree." My pulse pounded faster, echoing in my ears. "Besides, do you really think Mallory will let me be?"

"Hasn't she?"

"We all know she's probably just biding her time."

Archie snickered. "Don't tell me you think Mallory wants to kill you?"

"You're even more clueless than I thought you were." I gritted my teeth. "My toxic feud with Mallory isn't gonna end till one of us dies."

"That's a little morbid."

"Can't help if I call it like I see it."

He folded his arms. "What would your mother say if she could see you now?"

"Don't you dare bring up my mother."

"Not my fault you don't like what I have to say."

"My mother knew Mallory was a terrible person and that's all that matters."

"You're a good person, Chad. Don't be like this."

"Tell me something ... what do you think should happen to Mallory?"

"I don't know. But the one thing I do know is that it's not for you or I to decide what happens to Mallory. The universe will take care of her."

111

I cackled.

Archie gave me a confused look. "What's so funny?"

"Nothing."

"No, please share."

"You and I both know crime pays—otherwise nobody would do it."

"Whatever," Archie mumbled.

I sighed. "This conversation has ceased being productive. We're just talking in circles."

"So, what? You're just gonna walk away from me?"

"Yup," I said without even blinking.

His jaw trembled. "You know where to find me if you decide you want something different."

I darted away from Archie without another word. Getting sucked in by further conversation would've been pointless. Doing so would've wasted time. And no explanation necessary about how time was precious. It was the one thing I couldn't get back. Ezra and Mom proved that point all too well.

I bit my lip while turning right and entering the lot where I parked my car. A metallic taste soon filled my mouth. A part of me would never get used to Mom and Ezra being dead. The whole concept just seemed larger than life. One minute Mom and Ezra were alive. And the next they weren't. Haunting, really.

WEDNESDAY, MARCH 4

Gemma and I sat on my living room couch, sipping Cosmos. Alcohol wouldn't make my life perfect, but it could help ease the current knot in my stomach. My chat with Archie from the other day was still on my mind, in addition to how Gemma and I would have to make a decision sooner rather than later about how we'd finish Mallory once and for all.

Gemma giggled. "Cosmos were a great idea."

"No need to state the obvious, but I appreciate it." I took another swig of my drink, letting the cranberry flavor electrify my taste buds before I swallowed the contents. So, yeah. Life could've been worse. At least I wasn't drinking alone.

She let out a deep sigh. "I wanted to apologize to you."

My eyebrows scrunched. "For what?"

"Finding a doctor who will give sleeping pills isn't as easy as I thought it'd be."

"Don't worry about it."

"You don't have to put on a brave front on my account. You must be dying to wrap up our revenge against Mallory."

"These things can't be rushed."

"True. But it'd be nice to move on with our lives."

"Rushing things often leads to sloppiness."

"Touché." Gemma finished her Cosmo.

I meant what I said to Gemma and wasn't being polite just to save face. Finishing our scheme against Mallory was important. But Gemma and I had to be careful about how we wrapped things up. Mallory was a lot of things. However, she wasn't stupid. She successfully framed me for Kelly's murder, so I couldn't underestimate her. Planning several steps ahead was what a smart person did. Channeling the mind of a chess master entailed considering how Mallory might have more things up her sleeve.

A lump lingered in my throat. "Archie is like a dog with a bone."

"Huh?"

"I'm not joking. For whatever reason, he just won't give up on the idea of us reconciling. And I don't know what I'm gonna do."

Gemma tilted her head, looking me right in the eye. "What do you want to do?"

"Decimate Mallory once and for all." I fiddled with my fingers. "Love is a weakness I can't afford."

Her eyebrows shot up. "You're in love with Archie?"

Between Love and Death

"Don't put words in my mouth!" I quipped. "You know that's not what I meant."

"I wouldn't think less of you if you still cared about Archie."

"Thanks."

"I'm serious, Chad!"

"Duly noted."

Gemma patted my back. "You deserve to be happy."

In theory, I would've intellectualized Gemma's comment. Enjoying life would've been nice. But my life had been anything but simple since the start of junior year. Almost as if happiness was a foreign concept.

I stretched my arms. "I know. I know."

"Sometimes I wish we could rewind time."

"What are you getting at?"

Gemma pouted. "I wish Mallory never blackmailed Tommy to leave town."

"It is what it is."

A thought popped into my head and I suppressed laughter. Some thoughts were too morbid to mutter no matter how funny they might've been.

She gave me a confused look. "What? Do I have something in my teeth?"

"No, it's not that."

"Then what?" she asked, raising her voice slightly.

"It's not important."

"I deserve to know what's on your mind. Who knows. It might be able to help us in our quest to defeat Mallory."

"Don't say I didn't warn you."

Gemma continued making eye contact with me.

"You, Mallory, and I have all slept with Tommy."

I couldn't help myself regardless of how crude my comment was. Tommy sleeping with all three of us was something that actually happened. And I didn't know what to make of those odds. Lightning

114

striking twice was bizarre enough. But striking three times defied the odds.

She gaped. "I'm too sober for that realization."

"The thought never crossed your mind?" I asked.

"Never."

I chuckled. "If Tommy were still alive, then I wonder who he'd wanna be with."

"Not Mallory," Gemma blurted.

"You can really say that with complete certainty?"

"Yup." She pushed a lock of hair behind her ear. "It'd be nice to know once and for all if Kelly is dead."

"Come again."

"No need to be bashful. The thought must've crossed your mind once or twice about whether Kelly could still be alive."

"True."

"Murdering a sibling is a hell of a thing to do—even for someone like Mallory."

Gemma couldn't have said that. Showing Mallory any consideration—such as not being able to murder her own sister—was outrageous. Mallory was as cold-blooded as they came. And no doubt existed in my mind that Mallory would've robbed an elderly person if doing so would've benefited her.

My eyes bulged. "Did you just compliment Mallory?"

"I wasn't praising her. It was just an observation."

"Okay," I finally said. "Let's say for the sake of argument that Kelly is alive. What would you do with that information?"

She shrugged. "Don't know. Just something to consider."

MONDAY, MARCH 9

Rain drizzled while I exited the cemetery. I once again cursed the universe under my breath. This whole running into someone I didn't

Between Love and Death

want to interact with thing was getting old. Mallory was the last person I wanted to speak with. In fact, I would've rather conversed with the devil himself than come face to face with Mallory. And no. I wasn't exaggerating by believing the devil was the lesser of two evils. Any good will Mallory once had was long gone. Not that I was complaining or anything. Most friendships didn't last forever. And that was okay. The world would survive if Mallory and I didn't have the same dynamic that we had in middle school.

"What are you doing here?" she asked.

"Visiting my father's grave."

"What? Don't care about paying your respects to your mother?"

"Making assumptions about a situation you don't know anything about isn't a good look." The scowl intensified on my face. "Not that it's any of your business or anything, but I haven't gotten around to burying my mother's ashes."

"My mistake." Mallory batted her eyes. "Not gonna ask me what I'm doing here?"

"It's none of my business."

"How noble of you."

"I should get going."

Mallory grabbed my arm. "Wait!"

"What!" I bellowed, not even caring if anyone witnessed me raise my voice.

"It doesn't have to be this way."

"What are you babbling about now?" I demanded.

"Aren't you exhausted from the constant psychological warfare?"

"You started it, not me."

"That's a moot point now."

"Guess your ego couldn't take me rejecting you."

She beamed. "We could've been great together if you gave us a real chance."

"You can't bully someone into liking you, Mallory!"

116

Chris Bedell

"You really don't wanna know what I'm doing here?" Mallory drew in a deep breath. "Well, I'll tell you anyway … I'm paying my respects to Kelly."

I scratched an itch on the side of my neck. "If she's even dead, that is."

"What's that supposed to mean?"

I quirked my eyebrows. "It's not lost on me how Kelly could still be alive. Surely I don't need to remind you how the police never found her body?"

Mallory frowned.

"But I'll give you points for one thing," I said. "Having a tombstone is a nice touch."

"It's not a crime to have a grave for someone even if you don't have their remains."

"Never said it was." I stepped forward, practically invading Mallory's personal space. "So, how'd you do it? Did you blackmail Kelly into stockpiling enough of her blood so the police would rule her death a homicide despite there not being a body?"

Mallory winced.

"I mean, I already know you must have gotten my hair from a brush or comb that day you visited my mother to give her cookies," I continued.

"All you have is conjecture."

"But it's not nothing."

Mallory placed her hands on her hips. "Just be glad Gemma was able to bribe a judge so you could get out of jail."

"I don't need you to tell me what I should or shouldn't be thankful for."

"I'll let this conversation slide since not having any college prospects must suck. But I'd be very careful about how you proceed from here."

When I was right, I was right. I was the one who had the thought the other day about how I couldn't underestimate Mallory. And it looked

117

Between Love and Death

like I'd do well to pay attention to that idea. Losing to Mallory was the price of getting sloppy. And that couldn't happen. Not now. Not ever. Not when I was so close to defeating Mallory for good.

"I'm not afraid of you, Mallory!" I said.

"Maybe you should be."

I grinned. "I got you committed to a mental hospital once, and I can do it again."

"I'd like to see you try."

"You didn't have to be fixated on me … I'm sure you could've found a guy who would've been thrilled to go out with you."

"That's not the point and you know it."

"We never got a chance to dissect how humiliating it must've been to catch me in bed with Archie."

"Are you trying to piss me off?" Her hair shook in the wind. "If you are, then you're doing a good job."

"Archie still has it bad for me."

Just because I didn't want to reunite with Archie didn't mean I couldn't rub it in Mallory's face. And that was exactly what I'd do. It'd be different if my friendship with Mallory was salvageable, but it wasn't. That was like saying I could get blood from a stone. Mallory deserved every misfortune that came her way, including my gloating about how Archie was hung up on me and not her.

Mallory grumbled. "That's his problem."

"Not even a little jealous?"

"Nope … because I just realized something during the course of this conversation. You're gonna get what's coming to you one day, and I can't wait to toast a glass of champagne when that happens."

"You sound awfully confident about that."

A small smirk tugged at Mallory's lips. "The universe has a way of taking care of situations."

"I suppose you aren't gonna tell me if Kelly is really alive or not."

"If you're so smart, then you can connect the dots yourself."

Chris Bedell

"Someone sounds bitter. What's the matter? Don't tell me that you got rejected from all the colleges you applied to?"

"Hardly."

"Well, I'd tell you to have a good day, but we both know I wouldn't mean it."

WEDNESDAY, MARCH 11

Blue was waning from the afternoon sky while I played with the lock, almost cursing while trying to get the front door open. Although for all I knew, that could've been the universe's way of saying I needed to get a new front door.

The lock clinked and I entered my home. The only problem was I hadn't anticipated someone waiting for me on the living room couch when I got in. The man's menacing green eyes remained glued to me while my focus remained on the intruder. His appearance was polished enough. His black hair was slicked back in addition to how he sported a leather jacket, Polo shirt, khaki pants, and white sneakers.

"I suppose you must be wondering what I'm doing here?" asked the man.

How kind of the person to presume to know what I thought. As if that made the situation any easier.

"You have ten seconds to get out of my house before I call the police."

"I wouldn't do that if I were you." The man whipped out a gun from the inside pocket of his leather jacket and pointed it at me.

My back hairs rose while my breathing became more labored. Almost as if the room was spinning around me. After everything that happened to me, an intruder killing me couldn't be the way I was destined to die. The idea was nonsensical. Like saying apples and oranges were the same thing.

"I've got money," I stammered. "And lots of it. How would you like several million dollars?"

119

Between Love and Death

"This isn't about money. But I appreciate it, though."

The man's eyes remained on me while my throat tightened. The gun pointed at me should've been my only concern. Yet somehow, I wanted to laugh at the man's moustache. I hadn't noticed the guy's stereotypical porn moustache when I first entered my house. If I was being honest, then I needed to admit how the look was ridiculous. And if I wanted to be a wiseass, then I would've speculated how the man might've thought the porn moustache might make him better in bed.

"Any last words?" the man asked.

"You really don't want my money?" I asked, stuttering. "I can pull up my bank statement and prove how I'm not lying about being rich."

"I'm a closer. When someone hires me to do a job, I do it."

"Did Mallory hire you to kill me?"

"What kinda hitman would I be if I divulged who hired me?"

"Point taken."

Something clicked in my mind while the man's fingers remained on the gun. Perhaps my conversation with Mallory the other day was too close for comfort for her when I began poking around the Kelly question. The guess was as good as any even if I didn't have any concrete proof about Kelly being alive.

But if Mallory hired someone to kill me, then she was an even worse person than I thought.

"You shouldn't leave your front door unlocked, Chad."

I cocked my head. Archie just entered my house.

"You should go," I said.

Archie's gaze traveled to the living room. Then, he shifted his attention back to me. "Why is some intruder pointing a gun at you?"

"Just go!" I pleaded. "This doesn't involve you, Arch."

Archie gave me a weak smile. "Careful. I might think you care."

I resumed eye contact with the hitman. "Let Archie leave. He isn't a part of this."

120

The hitman huffed, fingers still on the trigger. "Killing a second person would complicate the matter."

"Exactly," I said.

Archie's lips quivered. "Wait. Did Mallory hire someone to kill you or something?"

I heaved a sigh. "Just leave, Archie!"

The man rose from the couch before heading towards me and Archie. His gun faced me and Archie the whole time while he approached us. Then, he shut the front door. "Didn't want anyone else to disturb us," he said.

I made a pig-like snort. "How kind of you."

"This ends now, goddammit!" Archie lunged at the hitman, sending the gun flying onto the floor. In fact, it was a miracle the gun didn't go off accidentally.

Archie and the hitman wrestled while numerous thoughts swirled in my mind. Mainly, how I needed to do something to help Archie. Archie was on the bottom and the hitman was on top. And I didn't know how much longer Archie could handle the him.

I grabbed the bookend on the table by the front door and clonked the hitman in the head several times. The man collapsed onto the ground and Archie stood.

"Thanks for that," Archie said.

"Don't mention it."

"We should call the police."

"That'd be a good idea."

"But seriously? We really think Mallory is behind this?"

"It's the only thing I can think of."

"Guess you forgot about me being a closer," the hitman said.

Archie and I tilted our heads at the same time. Somehow, the man had gotten ahold of the gun again. I could've kicked myself. I should've picked up the gun after smacking the man in the head with the bookend.

"You don't have to do this," I said.

Between Love and Death

The hitman's eyes lit up. "Oh, but I do."

"It's gonna be okay," Archie said.

"Adios, motherfucker!" The man pulled the trigger and Archie stepped in front of me. The bullet hit Archie in the chest.

My stomach sank. Just like that, the guy that I humiliated as part of my revenge scheme saved my life. I had no words, truly. Character wasn't just about doing something noble when nobody was paying attention. True character also encompassed doing something even when there wouldn't be praise for the deed.

"Archie, no!" I screamed.

The man collapsed onto the ground—perhaps he underestimated the full extent of his injury when I clocked him in the head.

I ran over to the hitman and picked up the gun before shooting the man three times. There was no way I'd let the man fire the gun again.

Heavy breathing echoed and I darted back towards Archie. His free hand remained on his chest, using his jacket to apply pressure. But if Archie was going to live, then I needed to call an ambulance ASAP.

"You're gonna be okay, Archie," I said after calling 911. "Just keep applying pressure. The ambulance should be here any minute."

He made brief eye contact with me, nodding.

THURSDAY, MARCH 12

I stood in the hallway outside Archie's room. In a twist of fate, Archie hadn't died on the way to the hospital or in surgery. To say I was relieved would be an understatement. Not wanting to reunite with Archie didn't mean I wanted unnecessary bloodshed in my war with Mallory. I didn't.

"He's in love with you," Andrea said. "I hope you know that."

I craned my neck. Somehow, I forgot it wasn't just me standing outside of Archie's hospital room. Archie's sister was with me while his mother was having a moment alone with her son. I prayed Andrea

Chris Bedell

wouldn't be too tough with me. There was no telling how much Archie might've told Andrea about everything that transpired since last June.

Andrea glared. "What? You have nothing to say?"

"Archie being alive is what matters."

"If you say so."

"I never wanted any of this to happen to Archie."

She sneered. "I find that hard to believe."

"And what's that supposed to mean?"

"I know about how you started sleeping with Archie again so you could arrange for Mallory to catch you two and subsequently dump Archie."

Welp. That answered my question.

I crossed my arms. "I don't have to justify my life to you."

"No, you don't. The only thing that matters is being happy with the person you see in the mirror. And I hope for your sake that you're pleased with the person you've become."

"Mallory is the one who hired a hitman to kill me."

"Whatever."

"You can't tell anyone. The official story is that I was a victim of a robbery gone bad."

"Guess you have everything figured out."

Archie's hospital room door opened. His mother, Doreen, closed the door behind her. Then she glanced at us.

"Archie is asking for you, Chad," Doreen said.

"Okay." I entered Archie's hospital room, being sure to close the door behind me.

"This is awkward." Archie laughed, then let out a loud cough.

"Save your energy."

"Just wanted to see how you were doing."

I gave him a mock frown. "You're the one who was shot."

"But there was no real damage. It's not like the bullet pierced my heart, lungs, or major arteries."

123

Between Love and Death

I fought back the tears in my eyes. Not because I was worried Archie might think there still might be a chance for us to reconcile, but because I needed to be strong for him. Archie needed the support, not me.

His gaze narrowed. "Just say whatever's on your mind."

"You saved me." I sighed while making sure to maintain eye contact. "And for that, I'll always be thankful."

"That's all you wanted to say?"

"Yeah."

FRIDAY, MARCH 20

Gemma, Archie, and I stood in my living room while I tried not to think about the grizzly scene that unfolded the previous week. My home being the place where Mom died was bad enough. But I couldn't believe that it was also the location of my almost-death.

Gemma flipped her hair over her shoulder. "No offense, Archie, but I'm having a hard time believing you want in on the plan to take down Mallory."

"Me almost dying changed things," Archie said. "Mallory is a cancer that must be eradicated. And the sooner the better."

"I knew you'd see it my way eventually," I said.

Archie clapped. "So, let's hear it then. I assume you and Chad have some ideas about how to defeat Mallory?"

"We do." Gemma cradled her hands behind her neck. "But any discussion about ending Mallory needs to include the possibility of Kelly still being alive. More specifically, about how we need to prove whether Kelly is dead or alive."

124

BEFORE

FRIDAY, AUGUST 23

I sat next to my lawyer, Sonia Drayton, in the courtroom while the prosecutor sat in her area as we continued waiting for the judge to arrive. With any luck, I'd make bail. I mean, I had to make bail. Not because I thought I was better than anyone else. But because I wasn't prepared to be in jail before I was even convicted. The idea was ludicrous, after all. It wasn't like I was a flight risk or anything. I wasn't.

Sonia leaned into my right ear. "It's totally normal for a judge to occasionally run late, so don't panic. Besides, I'm sure you'll make bail."

Relief should've pulsed through my body. My lawyer had a calming enough voice. I mean, she was one of the best attorneys in the state. But somehow my stomach coiled. Being in court meant my feud with Mallory had entered new territory. I wanted to curse the day Mallory was born. Mallory might've been a lot of things, however, I never once anticipated Mallory would best me. That was like saying a gazelle could beat a cheetah.

I tilted my head for a beat and made eye contact with Mom, who remained seated in the gallery. No denying how the world was a fucked-up place. But at least I had my mother. That was something. I

125

Between Love and Death

didn't know what I would've done if I had nobody besides my lawyer on my side. Nobody deserved to be alone during a crisis.

The only problem was that Mallory was also sitting in the gallery. I shuddered for the split-second we stole a shared gaze. Normally, someone grinning at me would've been a positive thing. But when Mallory was involved, I couldn't help wondering when she'd stick the next knife in my back. If I was being honest, then I needed to admit Mallory had me right where she wanted me. And it was going to take a miracle to get out of this predicament.

The judge entered the courtroom and everyone rose. She made her way to her spot and sat down in a matter of seconds.

"How does the defendant plead?" Judge Bell asked before blowing a loose strand of hair out of the way.

I forced a smile. "Not guilty, your honor!"

Judge Bell shifted her attention to the prosecutor. "And what are the people's thoughts on bail?"

Claire coughed into her right arm. "We'd like to ask that bail be denied, your honor. These are very serious charges, after all."

"I object to the opposing counsel editorialize things," Sonya said. "My client is well aware of how serious the matter is."

"Is he?" Judge Bell narrowed her gaze. "I mean, no offense or anything, but he's been charged with first degree murder."

I almost choked on the phrase "first degree murder." The situation had to have been a nightmare that I'd wake up from shortly. First degree murder was as serious as it got, so that wasn't exactly something that worked in my favor.

Sonia beamed. "I'm confident that the evidence will show that my client is innocent. The people are trying the case without a body."

Judge Bell glared at Claire.

"Yes, your honor," Claire said.

"Denying bail would be cruel," Sonia said.

"And why is that?" Judge Bell asked.

126

Sonia tugged at the sides of her gray blazer. "This is the first time my client has ever appeared in court."

"Duly noted," Judge Bell touted.

Claire shook her head. "If it weren't first degree murder, then sure. Maybe I'd be okay with bail. But that just isn't the case."

"It's not like my client is wealthy ... he's the last person who would charter a private jet to flee," Sonia said.

Judge Bell sighed. "Unfortunately, I'm inclined to agree with Ms. Hastings. Bail would be inappropriate due to the serious nature of the charges. The defendant shall be remanded to county jail for the duration of the trial."

I could only be strong for so long. And that was why I didn't even bother fighting back my tears. Not being able to catch a break—such as getting bail—made me want to scream. Anyone who was even halfway competent would realize I didn't fit the profile of a killer.

TUESDAY, SEPTEMBER 10

I sat in the visitor's room at the county jail, across from my mother. My current situation fucking sucked. But if this was the only way I'd be able to chat with Mom, then so be it. Besides, I needed to make the most of the time she had left. It wasn't lost on me how Mom could be dead by this time next year.

Mom gave me a weak smile. "How are you holding up, honey?"

"Terribly." I paused for a beat. "I'm sorry I can't be stronger. The whole situation is really messed up. And I blame Mallory for it."

"Yeah, I don't blame you."

I looked Mom over. It was the same woman I had known all my life sitting across from me. Yet something seemed different about her. Something I just couldn't put my finger on.

"How are you doing?" I asked.

"I have my good days and bad days."

127

Between Love and Death

"You aren't in pain, are you?"

"No, my doctors have that under control for the most part."

"That's good."

Mom leaned closer. "I didn't wanna have to bring this up. However, I don't think I have a choice since I could never forgive myself if anything happened to you."

"What are you talking about?"

"You've been keeping your head down, right?" Mom whispered. "I mean, there's nothing wrong with being unique. But this isn't the place to make a splash."

I shook my head. "No offense, but you're gonna have to be more specific."

"You need to focus on not getting raped."

"I'm sure there's worse jails to be remanded to before trial."

"That might be, but we can't be too careful. Not when your wellbeing is at stake? Do you understand me?"

"Yeah, I get it."

"Good. I'm glad." Mom's elbows slid onto the table. "I'm really not trying to upset you. It's just that someone like you could be an easy target."

"No explanation necessary."

"Maybe you could make friends with someone who could offer you protection."

"Are you suggesting that I pimp myself out so I don't get raped?"

"I didn't say you had to sleep with someone so they'd be your bodyguard." Mom exhaled a deep breath. "I just meant that it never hurts to have allies. You never know when it might come in handy. Especially in a place like this."

My throat burned. Life was complicated enough without contemplating if I was going to get raped while I passed my time waiting for my trial to start. The thought hadn't even crossed my mind until Mom brought it up. And now I wished she hadn't mentioned the

128

Chris Bedell

possibility of me getting sexual assaulted. There was no need to invent problems that didn't exist. When it came to worrying about rape, ignorance was bliss. The idea that someone could even be capable of that was maddening in and of itself.

Mom gave me a pleading look. "Please don't be angry with me. You know I only have your best interest at heart."

"I know," I lied.

Humoring Mom was best. I didn't have it in me to be mean to someone who had terminal cancer. If this was really the end for my mother, then I didn't want to have any regrets about the last period of her life. There was enough regret to go around as it was.

"What is it?" Mom asked.

I sobbed. "It was never supposed to be like this, Mom. If Mallory had never pursued Archie, then none of this would've happened."

"You can't change the past."

"Don't you think I know that?" I asked, cheeks burning. "Sorry. I didn't mean to lose my temper. I know you're only trying to help me."

"Already forgotten."

I raised my eyebrows. "Let's go back to your previous point … you don't really think I'll get raped, do you?"

"Probably not. But you have to stay vigilant."

"My cellmate is nice. He's only a year older than me."

"What's his name?"

"Ezra."

Mom ran her fingers through her hair. "It's not every day that you hear a name like that."

"No, it's not."

"Does he know about you?"

I stared Mom down. "Know what?"

"About you being bisexual?"

I shrugged. "If he does, then he hasn't said anything. I mean, he's given no indication to hint that he might be uncomfortable around me."

129

Between Love and Death

"Glad to hear it."

"Mallory is going to pay for this," I said, crying some more.

"Not so loud!" Mom quipped. "Raising anymore suspicion is the last thing you need to be doing."

"I can't help it." More tears fell down my face. "I'm pissed off as hell. And this situation isn't one that has an easy solution."

"I don't know how, but it'll be okay. Just hold onto that."

"Mallory is probably somewhere enjoying champagne."

"That doesn't matter." Mom bit her lip. "Just keep focusing on how the situation will be over before you know it."

"I don't understand how they even have a case if they don't have Kelly's body."

Mom scratched the side of her neck. "Yeah, the whole thing is bizarre. In all my years of watching cop shows, I never heard of a district attorney prosecuting a case without a corpse."

"I just thought of something else that makes the situation even worse," I blurted. "I'm gonna have to repeat my senior year of high school if I want a high school diploma. And while I'm at it, I might as well kiss college goodbye."

"That's the least of your worries." Mom fiddled with her cardigan. "Besides, you could always get your GED."

"True."

"Have you had any visitors besides me or Sonia?"

I whipped my head back and forth. Some truths were too difficult to articulate no matter how simple they were. Thinking Mom and my lawyer were the only people in my corner was a bitter pill to swallow. And I'd probably be better off if I didn't think about it.

The guard by the door hollered. "Time's up!"

"Remember what we discussed," Mom said.

"I know," I whispered.

130

Another guard approached me, then led me towards the exit. I took one last glance at Mom before we left the visitor room. Tears welled in my eyes while she nodded at me.

Yeah, it was official. I was in Hell. And it'd be a long time before my situation improved—if it did at all.

WEDNESDAY, SEPTEMBER 11

I was mopping the floors when a bald man with a goatee approached me. Three guys trailed behind him. My heart thumped faster and louder. All of my years of schooling couldn't have prepared me for this situation. On the one hand, I could acknowledge the man and his friends. On the other hand, I wasn't exactly sure what the proper etiquette was. Like if saying something might piss off the guy. And that was the last thing I wanted. Keeping a low profile was the way to go if I wanted to survive.

The bald man with a goatee gave me a toothy smile. "You could at least acknowledge me. I mean, what kind of dumbass motherfucker doesn't even say hello."

"My bad," I mumbled.

"I'm Fernando." He offered his hand and I shook it. Doing so seemed safe enough—Fernando was the one initiating the gesture, after all.

"Nice to meet you," I said.

"And that's Chip, Arthur, and Donald," Fernando said, pointing to each of his friends.

Sweat rolled down my back. "I don't mean to be rude or anything, but I should get back to mopping the floor. I wouldn't want one of the staff members to get mad at me."

Fernando's toothy smile expanded. "That's the thing about trouble. Sometimes, it finds you regardless of what you've done."

"What's that supposed to mean?" I asked.

Fernando snickered. "Just watch your back."

So much for worrying about not pissing anyone off. It was time to put my cards on the table and that was exactly what I'd do.

I wrinkled my nose. "That a threat?"

"Not at all," Fernando said. "It's just some friendly advice from one inmate to another."

"Well, thanks."

Fernando cackled. "Trust me ... you'd know if I wanted you dead. Nothing like stabbing someone with a shiv in the shower."

My body betrayed me because I winced without even considering how showing weakness wasn't a smart move. Not with a man like Fernando. He was easily a good six to eight inches taller than me, in addition to how he must've been a good fifty pounds heavier than me and decade older.

Fernando winked. "Guess I'll be seeing you around sometime."

"Sure thing." I resumed mopping.

Fernando and his gang strutted away from me and then they were soon out of sight. However, it took a good minute or two until it felt like my stomach was no longer in my throat. Getting into trouble when I was months away from my trial wasn't something that could happen. I needed to live long enough to prove my innocence. The only question that remained was if Fernando was just messing with me or if he actually had it out for me. If the universe wanted to be generous, then it'd be the former. But life was anything but fair, so I needed to be prepared for the latter.

WENDESDAY, SEPTEMBER 18

I lay in the bottom bunk, unable to sleep. I hadn't had a second encounter with Fernando. Yet the situation still resembled a ticking time bomb. My luck would run out eventually. That was the nature of situations, really.

"You'd do well to avoid Fernando," Ezra said from the top bunk.

Chris Bedell

I hopped out of the bunk and looked Ezra right in the eye. Having the conversation face to face was the only way to do it if we were going to discuss an issue as serious as Fernando.

"Excuse me?" I said.

"I'm not trying to upset you, Chad. I'm just being honest. I couldn't help noticing Fernando and his goons talking to you last week."

I stroked my chin. Ezra would make a good CIA recruit. I hadn't recalled seeing Ezra while I was chatting with Fernando. Yet Ezra had no reason to lie to me. There was nothing to gain from doing so.

Ezra sighed. "Fernando is a very dangerous man."

"Do I wanna know?"

"It's best if you do. He's on trial for a triple homicide."

"Come again?"

"You heard me. He's accused of killing his parents and brother."

"Why?" I stammered.

"I don't know, and it doesn't matter." Ezra got off the bunk bed, now standing only a couple of inches from me. "I mean this in the most delicate way possible, but someone like yourself would never be able to defend themselves against Fernando."

"Thanks for the vote of confidence."

"It has nothing to do with being weak. It's the truth."

"Whatever you say." I remained silent for a moment. "And just for the record, Fernando was the one who approached me."

"Still doesn't change how he's bad news."

I lifted my brow. "What's it to you?"

"Just trying to look out for you. I'd hate for something to happen to you."

"Really?"

"Yeah, a cute boy like yourself doesn't deserve whatever it is that Fernando might have planned for you."

Cute. The phrase lingered in my mind while I stood in silence and I refused to break eye contact with Ezra. If I didn't know better, then I'd

Between Love and Death

suspect Ezra just flirted with me. A guy complimenting another guy on his looks wasn't normal platonic behavior.

Ezra pulled me against his body after additional prolonged eye contact. However, I didn't push him off me or tell him to stop. I enjoyed every second of him massaging my mouth with his tongue.

So, it was safe to say that Mom and Sonia weren't the only ones on my side. Ezra was on Team Chad too. And for that I was thankful. Ezra was a good several inches taller than me, so he at least had that going for him when it came to dealing with Fernando.

MONDAY, SEPTEMBER 23

Mallory visiting me was the last thing I expected to ever happen. But as bad as Mallory was, I was getting a break by being in the visitor room. And besides, sitting across from each other allowed for a little distance.

I snickered. "Let me guess. You came here to gloat."

"You know me well."

"Let's cut the bullshit and be honest with each other."

She twirled a strand of hair around her finger. "Sure, I can do that for you."

"You and I both know I didn't kill Kelly," I said. "Not to mention, you look awfully calm for someone whose sister was brutally murdered."

"And what's that supposed to mean?"

"Either you killed Kelly or you pressured her into staging her own death." I beamed. "Just can't get over how the police never found a body."

"You have a very active imagination."

"It's the truth."

Mallory gave me a wry smile. "Tell yourself whatever you need to sleep at night."

"You aren't gonna get away with this."

134

Chris Bedell

"Looks like I already did."

My eyes bulged. "That a confession?"

"What do you think?"

"Answering a question with another question is kinda pathetic."

"I didn't realize you were the grammar and syntax police."

"Does Archie know you came to visit me today?" I demanded.

Mallory nodded. "He does. And he's very disappointed in you, Chad. He had high hopes you'd turn your life around."

Please. As if I needed to listen to Mallory lecturing me. No thanks. Hell would freeze over before I'd ever consider Mallory a paragon of virtue. In fact, I'd even go as far as to say Mallory was the least noble person I've ever met.

"Whatever," I mumbled.

"Remember when you visited me at the sanitarium back in April?"

"Yeah, I do."

"Well, the tables have turned since then."

"Better be careful, sweetheart. One day you're gonna say the wrong thing and incriminate yourself."

"I'm doing just fine."

"Your victory won't last forever."

Mallory leaned closer, so close the guard gave a dirty look. "You're right ... I framed you for Kelly's murder and there isn't a fucking thing you can do about it."

Lunging towards Mallory might've been the type of overreaction she was hoping for. So, I wouldn't fall for her goading me. Keeping a low profile wasn't only about avoiding people like Fernando. I couldn't do anything that'd get me charged with additional crimes. That was a guaranteed way to make sure I'd never leave prison.

WEDNESDAY, SEPTEMBER 25

I was in the breakroom, enjoying a rare break when Fernando and his goons walked in. Noticing things from the corner of my eye and not drawing attention to the observation was just something I was going to have to get used to if I wanted to survive being remanded to county jail.

Fernando whistled as he approached me. "The breakroom guard is on a smoke break, so that gives us a few minutes to ourselves."

I looked up from my game of solitaire. "I see."

Fernando clapped. "You know what to do, boys!"

Two of them grabbed me, each taking an arm. The third man removed my shirt, exposing my chest and back.

"Are you going to rape me?" I asked, fear pulsing through my veins.

If something terrible was going to happen to me, then I at least deserved a head's up so I could prepare myself.

Fernando chuckled. "Not at all—I'd never violate someone like that. Rape is the worst thing you can do to a person. I just like to think of this as a little initiation. I promise it'll only hurt a little. Fuck, maybe I'll even give you a kiss to make it feel better."

Fernando whipped out a cigarette lighter from his pocket. I'd save my breath by not questioning how he could get that. Doing so would've wasted time ... time I didn't have. The emptiness grew inside me while I cursed the universe under my breath for being so cruel to me. Life was pretty fucked up when you had to question whether being burned with a cigarette lighter was worse than being raped.

He clicked the cigarette lighter, then burned my back with it. I screamed, realizing nobody was there to witness my cry for help, which was beyond tragic. I could only depend on myself and I wasn't enough.

WEDNESDAY, OCTOBER 2

I exhaled a deep breath while Ezra and I stood in our cell. "I don't want to go into the details, but you were right about Fernando."

Chris Bedell

"Sorry to hear."

"It'll be fine."

"You can tell me what happened to you. I promise I won't think any less of you because Fernando and his gang bested you in some way." Ezra grimaced. "Did Fernando and his goons rape you or something?"

"No, but I wish they had."

Ezra gave me a confused look.

"Fernando burned me with a cigarette lighter," I continued.

Ezra clapped his hand over his mouth.

I stomped my feet. "I hate it here!"

"You and me both."

I collapsed into Ezra's chest and he hugged me from behind. I couldn't help the feeling of wanting to cry into a pillow. My life had become so pathetic that getting comfort from a stranger was as good as it got.

"Eventually, Fernando's behavior will catch up to him," Ezra said.

"If only life were that simple."

I stepped away from Ezra.

"You don't believe in karma?" Ezra asked.

"I want to, but it's hard."

"That's understandable. Maybe we should change the subject."

"Good idea." My heart fluttered a little. Like it or not, a certain novelty existed with Ezra. He was something new and exciting. And when I was in Hell, I needed anything positive I could find. Life just had to be good again. I refused to believe that my best days were behind me. I was only eighteen, after all. My whole life was ahead of me. And Mallory wouldn't win. She couldn't. I had been through a lot already, so I'd get through my current predicament. Even if the situation was less than ideal. "I'm not gonna beat around the bush. I haven't been able to stop thinking about the kiss. And if it's okay with you, I'd like to express just how much I'm enjoying having you as my cell mate."

He smirked. "Wow."

137

Between Love and Death

I glanced at Ezra's waist, then resumed eye contact. Ezra nodded. I kneeled while Ezra slipped out of his pants and underwear. I was about to give someone a blow job in less than ideal conditions. But I didn't care. I just wanted to dull my mind and numb the pain. Something, anything, to make me forget how unfair life was.

WEDNESDAY, OCTOBER 9

I sat across from Sonia at a table in the visitor's room. And I hated to admit it, but the visit was a welcomed distraction. Perhaps Sonia had an update about how preparing for trial was going. At this rate, I just needed something. Anything that might've hinted that I had a chance at winning my case.

"How are you doing?" I asked.

Sonia coughed into her right arm. "I'm sorry to have to do this to you, but there's no easy way to say this. Your mother died."

"What?" I said, stuttering.

"She passed away yesterday afternoon."

Tears pricked my eyes—I must've misheard Sonia. My mother couldn't be dead. She had to make it through at least the end of the year. So yeah, Sonia would clear up the confusion any second now. I was sure of it.

"Her doctor overestimated how much time she had left," Sonia continued.

"This has to be a joke."

"I'm afraid not."

"My mom can't be dead!" I wailed.

"Apparently, she'd been feeling weaker than she let on."

"Fuck!" I mumbled under my breath.

"As tragic as your mom dying is, it doesn't change anything. I'm still representing you pro bono, so don't even worry about money."

"That's great."

138

Chris Bedell

"It won't be hard to poke holes in the prosecution's case." Sonia rubbed the back of her neck. "It all goes back to how they don't have a body."

I might as well have been sucked up into a tornado because I couldn't help tuning out Sonia while she droned on. Time hadn't been on my side. Cancer had caught up to Mom. And now she was gone.

I wouldn't forget Mom, though. I couldn't. Her blood literally ran through my veins, so Mom was with me even when she wasn't with me.

AFTER

WEDNESDAY, APRIL 1

I exited a pizza shop on Main Street, making sure the box was level while I carried it. And it wasn't long until I ran into Doreen. She just exited the pharmacy, which was a couple of shops down from SILVIO'S PIZZA. I wasn't sure if I should smile or frown while Archie's mother stood in front of me. To say my situation with Archie was complicated was an understatement. On the one hand, I couldn't deny how my feelings for Archie weren't black and white. In a perfect world, there would've been no Mallory drama and we would've been together. On the other hand, a lot had transpired since the first day of junior year. And I couldn't forget about it as much as I wished I could snap my fingers and erase all the unpleasant events.

Doreen grinned. "Hi, Chad."

"How are you doing?"

"Do you want a real answer?"

"You can be as honest as you want." I paused for a moment, once again making sure I didn't drop the pizza box. It was heavier than it looked. "I mean, it must be such a relief that Archie is okay."

140

Chris Bedell

She giggled. "I'm not clueless despite how long it's been since I was a teenager."

"Pardon me?"

"I know there's more going on. Only an idiot would be oblivious about how something fucked up is going on."

My pulse drummed in my ears. Surely, Archie hadn't told his mother all the gory details of the last seventeen months. Confiding in his sister was one thing—she was a peer, not an authority figure. But I didn't know what I'd do if Doreen became privy to everything. At the end of the day, Archie joined "Operation Takedown Mallory." And Archie should've been smart enough to know telling his mother the truth would've meant adding another variable to the situation, which was something we couldn't afford to do regardless of how nice Doreen was. Life needed to get less complicated, not more complicated. The fewer people that knew about wanting to destroy Mallory the better.

Doreen chewed on the inside of her lip. "Relax, dear. Archie didn't betray your confidence or anything. I just have good intuition."

"I see."

"If something is going on, then you should tell me. It doesn't matter if being eighteen means you're legally an adult."

"You wouldn't understand."

"Try me."

"It was nice of you to visit me in prison that day last fall," I said, doing my best to change the subject. Hopefully, Doreen would be gullible enough to take the bait. I mean, it wasn't like I asked for diamonds or a mansion. I just didn't want to make my life more complicated than it needed to be.

"I'm not dropping this."

So much for the universe doing me any favors.

"I'm not sure what you want me to say," I finally replied.

"I only wanna help. I'm not trying to bust you or anything."

"It's better if you don't know."

141

Between Love and Death

Her jaw twitched. "It's about Mallory, isn't it?"

My eyes widened. "What would make you say that? Mallory hasn't done anything to you, has she?"

Doreen wrinkled her nose. "No, she hasn't. But the reality is that I never got a good vibe from her."

"Really?"

"Some people just give off bad energy. And I don't care if that sounds negative—it's the truth."

"It's important that you stay away from Mallory." I drew in a breath. "You'll be better off if you do."

"Okay. Fine. I'll take your word for it."

"I'm really not trying to be difficult here. It's just better if you're in the dark. I mean, knowledge isn't always power."

"I appreciate that." Doreen pursed her lips. "The whole thing never seemed right with how the police were never able to find Kelly's body. I'm sure you don't think she's actually dead, do you?"

"It doesn't matter what I think. The only thing that matters is what I can prove."

"Fair enough."

"If you don't mind me asking, did you spend a lot of time with Mallory?"

"Not much. But it was enough to know she was bad news."

I gritted my teeth. "She only pursued Archie to get revenge against me."

Not being able to tell Doreen everything that was going on didn't mean she had to be completely in the dark. I could fill in some details for Doreen. Nothing too damning. Just enough information to drive home the point about that Mallory was dangerous.

"That doesn't surprise me," Doreen said.

"We're talking about someone who will stop at nothing to get what she wants."

"I'm just glad Archie is free of her."

142

Chris Bedell

"You and me both."

Her face drooped. "It sucks that you never got to enjoy your senior year of high school."

"It is what it is."

"That's a mature attitude of you to have. I'd be pissed off if I were you."

"The past already happened. The future is the only thing I can control."

"I guess so." Doreen squealed. "Did Archie tell you that he got an acceptance from Dafton University?"

Brief euphoria flooded my body. I could still be happy for Archie even if we weren't officially dating. I could only run from the truth for so long. More specifically how Archie hadn't turned against me because of his own doing. Like it or not, Mallory was the one who staged it so Archie would overhear my confession about how I framed her for Tommy's murder and was thus responsible for ending up in the mental hospital. It wasn't like Archie wanted to cause me pain because he was a mean person. No, that was Mallory's department.

The happiness lingered in my body for another beat. Dafton University might not have been on the opposite side of the country, but it was still a fresh start. And with a little luck, college would be less dramatic for Archie than high school was. Intense drama was best left where it belonged—in television shows and movies. Watching a hyper-reality was one thing, but living a larger than life situation was a different story.

I whipped my head back and forth. "No, he didn't. But that's great."

"He'll only be fifteen minutes away."

"You must be happy about that."

Doreen squealed louder. "You have no idea. I mean, no offense to Andrea or anything, but Archie has always been the good one. I don't know what I'd do without him."

143

Between Love and Death

A part of me couldn't believe what Doreen confessed. Parents weren't supposed to favor one child over another. Doing so would've been unfair. But I couldn't blame Doreen for her logic. Not entirely, at least. If I had two children, and one of them caused trouble while the other flew under the radar, then I'd favor the quieter one.

I let out a small laugh. "Hopefully, Andrea isn't causing too much trouble."

"Not anymore."

"That's good to hear."

"You sure there isn't anything I can do for you, dear?" Doreen asked.

Caring was sweet, but the further Doreen got from the Mallory situation, the better. I'd never be able to live with myself if Doreen became a pawn in my toxic feud with Mallory. Nothing good ever came from innocent people being harmed.

"No, I'm good." I gripped the pizza box tighter. "But thanks. Most people don't care."

"That's a shame."

I pushed down the lump in my throat. "I appreciate your support and all, but you should know something. I'm not perfect."

"Never thought you were."

"I've made mistakes."

Doreen sighed. "I'm sure I don't need to tell you how Archie cares a lot about you."

"No, you don't." I gave Doreen an apologetic look. "I don't mean to be rude, but I should get going. The pizza is probably cold by now."

Chatting with Doreen for a few minutes was one thing. However, I didn't have all night. So, the sooner I returned home, the better. I also couldn't imagine that Doreen wanted to chat with me for the next several hours. She must've had better things to do.

She jabbed her fist through the air. "Crap. I guess what my husband said about me never shutting up is true."

"Don't worry about it. It's not a big deal."

144

Doreen locked eyes with me. "You and Archie can still end up together. If you want to, that is."

"Thanks. I'll take that under advisement."

"That's all I can ask."

"But I'm serious about you having nothing to do with Mallory and how the less you know the better. She's poison."

"Duly noted."

FRIDAY, APRIL 3

Archie and I sat in my dining room, enjoying Chinese food. Somehow, I agreed to have a date with Archie.

Archie smirked. "This is nice, don't you think?"

"There are worse ways to spend a Friday evening."

"Shut up!" he exclaimed. "You know you're enjoying the date."

"So, that's what this is?"

"Playing hard to get isn't a good look."

"Sorry if I can't be better company. Just wish we were able to get a concrete lead on the Kelly situation. Knowing whether she is alive or dead would help."

"There are other ways to mess with Mallory besides knowing if Kelly is actually dead or not."

"I ran into your mother the other day." I ate another spoonful of rice. "She really is a lovely woman."

"No need to state the obvious. But thanks, I appreciate it." Archie guzzled more soda, then burped. "Sorry."

"Don't mention it."

"There's a point to my story."

"Okay, I'm listening."

"I'm sure I don't need to tell you how your mother can't be involved in the Mallory situation. It's for her own good."

"I know. I know."

145

Between Love and Death

Tears almost dotted my eyes. "And I don't mean to get sappy or anything, but that really is incredible how you took a bullet for me."

"I would've done that for anyone."

"I was using my anger as an excuse to hide my feelings for you," I said.

Archie looked up from his chicken and garlic sauce. "Where's this coming from?"

"You deserve to know the truth. You did save my life and all."

"No offense, but I don't want you to be with me out of pity."

Archie should've known better than to make that kind of comment. I was a lot of things, but nobody forced me to do something I didn't want to. I was a big boy. And if I didn't want to associate with Archie, then I wouldn't. But that clearly wasn't the case. It didn't take much for me to be talked into having dinner with Archie. Like it or not, Archie proved he was a good person when he took that bullet. It didn't matter how much time went by since that fateful day. Archie getting shot would forever be etched in my mind. I mean, in an ideal situation, it wouldn't have taken such an extreme event for my dynamic with Archie to thaw. But the point is that the hostility is no longer there. The only question that remained was what I was going to do with this second chance with Archie.

"It's not about that." I scarfed down more rice. "It's just about how the anger kept me going. Mallory deserves to be hated after everything she's done to me. Although, you didn't deserve to become a target for my anger."

"Thanks." Archie took a napkin and wiped sauce from his lip. "However, I owe you an apology, too."

I furrowed my eyebrows. "For what?"

"I shouldn't have let Mallory turn me against you. You didn't deserve that. I've come to realize life isn't always black and white."

"That's big of you to admit."

"It's the truth."

Chris Bedell

I almost choked on the lump in my throat. "And I can't forget about how I got caught up in the fantasy."

"What are you getting at, Chad?"

"I'm talking about Ezra."

Archie gaped. "Oh."

"It sounds cliché ... because it is. Although, that doesn't change how Ezra was supposed to be my fresh start."

"Were you in love with him?"

"It was easy."

"I see."

"The reality is that I needed an ally in jail. And Ezra was mine." I took another bite of the chicken and garlic sauce. "But that doesn't mean what Ezra and I had wasn't real."

"Fair enough."

"Guess what I'm trying to say is that if we're gonna have any hope of working out, then we need to take things slow."

"Understood. But again, I need to be honest with you." He averted his gaze. "I don't want you to be with me because you're settling."

"I'm not."

"It seems like me taking a bullet changed things between us, though."

"It was a catalyst, yes. But I never stopped thinking you were attractive."

Archie patted my hand. "You really didn't deserve what Mallory did to you."

"Anyway, I hear congrats are in order. You must be excited about getting into Dafton University?"

He grunted. "I'm gonna kill my mother."

"Don't be so uptight. It's natural for a parent to wanna brag about their child. I wish my mother was still alive to brag about me."

147

And there it was. Mom. As much as I tried, I couldn't outrun Mom. Being dead didn't mean she wouldn't still come up in conversation. She would. And that was fine. Mom deserved to be remembered.

Archie stared me down. "Just want you to know that you can discuss your mother anytime you want. You don't have to worry about being a buzzkill or anything."

"Great. I'll keep that in mind"

SATURDAY, APRIL 4

I was in the middle of grocery shopping when I bumped into Rebecca and Dan. And if I was being honest with myself, then I needed to admit I wasn't sure how I was supposed to feel about crossing paths with Rebecca and Dan. Softening my opinion about Archie was one thing. But I knew Archie in ways I didn't know Rebecca and Dan. And that begged the question of what hurt more ... being disappointed by a lover or being disappointed by a friend. If Dan and Rebecca were really my friends, then they should've risen above Mallory's antics and had my back no matter what.

Rebecca grinned. "Nice to see you, Chad."

"I could say the same, but I won't lie," I said.

Dan winced. "Ouch."

"The world will survive if we don't repair our friendship." My hands remained on the shopping cart.

"I got into Yale," Rebecca blurted. "And Dan got into Brown."

I feigned a smile. "Isn't that something."

"We aren't idiots," Dan said.

I raised my brow. "Come again?"

"The past doesn't have to define us," Dan said.

"I don't need you to tell me what I already know, but thanks," I said.

Rebecca scowled. "So you can be on better terms with Archie, but not us? Why is that?"

148

Chris Bedell

I scoffed. "It's none of your business. That's what that is."

"It doesn't have to be this way!" Dan pleaded.

I sneered. "Forgive me for sounding trite, but you and Rebecca are a day late and a dollar short. As usual, you have no idea what's going on."

Rebecca's jaw lowered slightly. "And what the hell does that mean?"

"I probably shouldn't be telling you this, but at this point I've run out of fucks to give." I remained silent for a moment. "Remember the day an intruder broke into my house and shot Archie? Well, the man was really a hitman Mallory hired."

Rebecca blinked. "What?"

"I shit you not," I said.

"How can you be certain?" Dan pushed his glasses up.

"The man all but admitted to it," I said. "Besides, I found Mallory's number in his contacts."

Rebecca rubbed her temple. "Wow. I had no idea."

I huffed. "So, if you two wanna act like bumbling idiots, then that's your business. But do me a favor and leave me alone."

"Guess Mallory is a psycho," Rebecca said to Dan.

Dan glared at me. "What are you gonna do about Mallory?"

"That's for me to know and you to find out," I said. "But you can rest assured that I'm not gonna let the situation go."

Rebecca snort-laughed. "I wouldn't expect anything less."

"If you two know what's good for you, then you'll keep your distance from Mallory." I checked the time on my iPhone.

TUESDAY, APRIL 7

Gemma, Archie, and I stood in my kitchen while déjà vu overcame me. There wasn't anything I could do about the feeling, though. Life was going to be like this for the foreseeable future while the three of us continued plotting against Mallory.

149

Between Love and Death

Sorrow colored Gemma's face. "I really am sorry about how my PI wasn't able to find anything useful about Mallory."

"It's fine." I tucked my hands behind my neck. "It would've been naïve to expect Mallory to lead us right to Kelly."

"If she's still alive, that is," Archie interjected.

Gemma ran her fingers through her hair. "At this point, I'd bet my life on Kelly still being alive. The police usually find some sort of remains."

"We're gonna have to adjust the plan," I finally said.

Gemma's eyes bulged. "Does that mean you wanna fake a reconciliation with Mallory so you can start drugging her with the sedatives so she blacks out and is re-committed to the mental hospital because of being a danger to herself?"

"It's bigger than that," I said.

Archie chuckled. "You're gonna have to be more specific, babe."

"Getting Mallory re-committed to the sanitarium is a temporary solution at best," I confessed. "She'd get released one day."

"Then what are you suggesting?" Gemma asked, raising her voice.

I rubbed my hands together. "I'm gonna give Mallory the one thing she's always wanted ... me. And then I'll eventually kill her and make it look like a suicide."

Archie's Adam's apple throbbed. "Wow."

"Desperate times call for desperate measures." I poured myself a glass of water, then took a more than generous sip of it. "I mean, imagine what it'd be like to live in a world without Mallory. Wouldn't that be great"

"You're comfortable with cold-blooded murder?" Gemma asked.

I cackled. "Not like we're targeting an innocent grandma. Mallory deserves to be decimated. Have you forgotten how I would've never been burned with a cigarette lighter or almost beaten to death if she hadn't framed me for Kelly's murder?"

"Chad does have a point," Archie said.

Gemma nibbled on the inside of her lip. "It's not that I'm having second thoughts or anything. It's just that pretending to date Mallory only so you can kill her is a dangerous game. What if she catches onto you? Mallory is a lot of things, but she isn't stupid."

I sighed at them. "It's a risk I have to take. There's only two months left in the school year, so we're running out of time."

WEDNESDAY, APRIL 8

I took several deep breaths while I stood outside Mallory's front door, working up the nerve to ring the doorbell. My life would be okay. Cozying up to Mallory was just a natural part of the plan. It wasn't like I wanted to sleep with Mallory. No, I wouldn't let the situation get that far. I couldn't. I wouldn't want to have sex with Mallory if she were the only other person left on Earth. In fact, even thinking about being intimate with Mallory was enough to give me goosebumps. Marriage wasn't required in order to be intimate with someone. However, there was something to be said about needing to trust the person I was sleeping with.

Enough stalling. Time to ring the doorbell.

The door opened after another beat, revealing Mallory.

"What are you doing here?" she asked.

Rain drizzled against the ground. But not even bad weather would stop me from my mission. This conversation with Mallory was about the greater good, and I'd forever remain focused on that idea.

I pressed my hands together. "Do you have a moment to talk? I promise not to take up too much of your time."

She heaved a sigh. "Fine."

Mallory stepped outside after closing the door behind her. Interesting. She wasn't inviting me into her home.

"What's up?" Mallory asked.

Between Love and Death

"I owe you a big apology. I've been lying to myself big time, and that ends today. I've been in love with you for the longest time."

"What the fuck?"

"I'd be shocked, too, if I were you."

She narrowed her gaze. "Where's this coming from?"

"I was afraid to date you because I didn't wanna ruin our friendship. So, I decided to hide behind hostility and resentment."

"Wow!" she exclaimed.

"We've always had a natural chemistry between us."

"I won't argue with that."

"It won't be easy, but I'm willing to turn the page if you are. I mean, our situation would be the very definition of a romantic trope."

"How so?"

"Friends to enemies to lovers is kinda tropey, don't you think?"

"Yeah, I guess you have a point." Mallory remained silent for a beat. "Anyway, I appreciate your honesty. But what gives? No offense, but I can't help but wonder where this revelation came from."

"The day the intruder broke into my house and almost killed me changed things." I maintained eye contact with Mallory. Doing so was the only way to sell the story I was giving her. "I could've died, but I didn't. So, I'm gonna start living my life differently. We can put an end to this toxic feud. If you want to, that is."

She folded her arms. "What about Archie?"

"He's just a friend."

"You're on speaking terms with him again?"

"Yeah, I needed to let go of the anger. Surely you can appreciate that?"

"I can."

"So, what do you say? Why don't you make me the luckiest guy in the world and give a relationship with me a real shot?"

"Sure. But let's seal it with a kiss."

"Okay…"

152

"That won't be a problem, will it?"

I didn't waver. "Nope."

Kissing Mallory was one of the last things I wanted to do. But I would tolerate the fleeting moment of panic if making out with Mallory meant I was one step closer to destroying her.

"Oh, for fuck's sake," Mallory said. "Guys these days are way too timid about making the first move."

Mallory pulled me against her body before I could blink. And before I knew it, her lips pressed against mine. But I had nothing to worry about. I felt nothing for Mallory.

MONDAY, APRIL 20

Archie grinned at me while we stood in my bedroom after I locked the door. I couldn't take the risk of Gemma stumbling upon an intimate moment between Archie and I. Even if Gemma said she'd be out for most of the evening. After everything that transpired since the beginning of junior year, I wasn't about to leave anything to chance.

Archie's smirk deepened. "Are we really gonna do this?"

"Yeah, why? Do you have second thoughts?"

"Not at all."

Archie kissed me and what unfolded next could be compared to someone riding a bike after several years of not doing so. Every neuron in my body became electrified while I inhaled the mixture of the sweet and herbal aroma of whatever deodorant Archie used.

The kisses grew more vigorous while we shed our clothes faster than I could count to three.

Archie looked down at me while I cocked my head. "Sure you wanna do this, Chad? I'm fine with just making out."

Giving me an out was sweet. But I didn't need Archie to protect me. If I didn't want to sleep with someone, I wouldn't. But that wasn't the

Between Love and Death

case here. Archie and I were going to give in to desire. And there wasn't anything anyone could do about it.

It was my turn to smirk. "There's nothing I want more."

Archie lowered his body and his fingers became linked with mine. It wasn't long before I closed my eyes, allowing myself to get lost in the tryst. Archie and I didn't have forever, but we had this moment, and that was enough. By some miracle, Archie broke down my walls. I wouldn't have it any other way.

WEDNESDAY, APRIL 22

Andrea approached me after I got a latte from the coffee cart in the park. A humid breeze even trickled through the air. There was no debate to be had about it. It was truly spring.

"Nice to see you," I said.

The blank expression remained plastered on Andrea's face. "Wish I could say the same about you."

"If you have a problem with me, then at least have the guts to say it to my face. That'd be the decent thing to do."

"I can't control Archie," Andrea said.

"I'm not following."

"Not being able to tell Archie what to do and liking his choices are two different things. If you hurt Archie again, I'll kill you."

"Lovely."

Andrea seethed. "My mother might be drinking the Kool-Aid about you and Archie, but I'm not. I have my eye on you two."

"Alrighty then."

"I'm not afraid of you."

"Did I give you a reason to be scared of me?" I asked.

"Archie deserves to be happy."

"No argument there."

"Just don't fuck it up this time."

154

Chris Bedell

Getting annoyed with Andrea would've wasted both time and energy. I mean her behavior was cute in a way. Her protectiveness about Archie showed she cared, which was something that couldn't be said about all siblings.

I prayed Andrea didn't vent her frustration to the wrong person, though. Having Mallory discover Archie and I were secretly dating while I was wooing her was the last thing I needed. With Mallory's unstableness, there was no telling what might happen.

BEFORE

FRIDAY, NOVEMBER 1

Having sex while I was remanded in county jail before my trial was one of the few good things I had going for me. That was why I closed my eyes while resting my head on Ezra's chest. Sure. Eventually, we'd have to go back to the monotony of our routine. However, that didn't mean I couldn't enjoy myself. Fernando and his goons hadn't accosted me since Fernando burned my back with the cigarette lighter. But I'd forever be on guard. That was just the reality of my life. That meant predicting when the next bad thing might happen. It was worth a try, at least. I refused to lose to either Mallory or the universe.

Ezra getting a bottle of lube was impressive. That wasn't something I expected someone to get in prison. Yet Ezra did, and I'd be forever thankful for it. I wouldn't have been able to go all the way with Ezra without the bottle of lube. There was no way I was using spit for that. This was real life, not porn. And that meant I had to have some standards regardless of how hormones might've influenced me.

Ezra sighed. "This is something, isn't it?"

"Yeah, it is."

156

Chris Bedell

"I don't mean to sound corny, but I'm glad we found each other." He paused for a beat. "If I'm being honest, then I need to admit how you're the first good thing to happen to me in a long time."

"Same."

"I hope you enjoyed yourself."

"I'm just amazed how we both fit on the bottom bunk."

Ezra chuckled. "I won't lie. It's definitely a tight squeeze."

"There's something I need to say, so please don't accuse me of being negative or inventing problems that don't exist."

"Okay. Shoot."

"You don't think Fernando will come after me again, do you?"

"Why do you ask?"

"Can't help it."

"Hopefully, it's a good sign that you haven't had any more run-ins with him," Ezra finally said.

"Yeah, I'm sure everything will be fine."

"Do me a favor, though."

"Okay?"

"Don't bring up Fernando right after we have sex. That isn't exactly the pillow talk I was hoping for—no offense or anything."

When Ezra was right, he was right. I should've been smarter than to mention Fernando right after having sex. My connection to Ezra wasn't something that could be tainted by Fernando. And that was the way it needed to stay.

I laughed. "None taken."

"What's your favorite memory from before you arrived here?"

I bit my lip. "I don't know."

Ezra exhaled a deep breath. "Fine. I'll share if you can't think of one. My favorite memory before I got here is my fifth birthday."

"Why?"

157

"My father was out of town, so it was just Mom and me," Ezra said, voice cracking. "We went to a local carnival and then to the Olive Garden for dinner."

"Sounds like a lot of fun."

"Forgetting my birthday was the kindest thing my father could do for me." Ezra squeezed me tighter.

Ezra's comment made my heart hurt. My reasoning had nothing to do with being dramatic. The subtext spoke for itself. So, I wouldn't press Ezra further unless he wanted to discuss his father or his childhood. If Ezra was going to address his trauma, then he needed to do it for himself. Not because I badgered him into it.

"That sounds morbid," I whispered.

"It's the truth."

"Relax. I believe you."

"You really can't think of one good memory from before you were remanded here?"

"Probably something related to my mother before her cancer diagnosis."

"It's okay if you wanna discuss your mom. I promise not to judge."

"Thanks. I appreciate it."

Knowing Ezra meant well and taking him up on his offer were two different things. Mom would always be with me. But the less I thought about Mom, the better. I needed to be strong in a place like this. Like it or not, losing my mother to cancer at eighteen was a weakness that someone could exploit. I couldn't have that. I didn't know how, but I was going to get out of this hellhole alive.

FRIDAY, NOVEMBER 8

Footsteps squeaked, growing louder with each passing second while I played solitaire with a deck of cards at a table in the breakroom.

Chris Bedell

Someone cackled. I titled my head. Unfortunately for me, Fernando just shuffled into the room.

"Long time no see," I said.

Fernando snickered. "I was just thinking to myself how I haven't seen you in such a long time. And then bam ... I run into you. What a coincidence."

"You're lucky I didn't report you to the staff."

He snorted. "Please, you don't have the guts."

"Why do you hate me so much?" I demanded, anger bubbling inside me. "It's not like I ever did anything to you."

"When did I ever mention disliking you?"

"Burning my back with a cigarette lighter suggests animosity, don't you think?"

"It was a ritual."

"Does picking a fight with someone weaker than you make you feel like a real man?"

His gaze narrowed. "Are you saying you aren't as strong as me?"

"You know what I meant."

Fernando grabbed the cards from my hand, then threw them into the distance. After that, he scattered the remaining cards on the floor.

I stood. "So, we're really gonna do this?"

"You tell me."

"You're the one who seems ready to fight."

"Because I'm gonna beat the living shit out of you."

Fernando head butted me before I could so much as even catch my breath. I collapsed onto the ground while an ache jolted through my head. Then, Fernando kicked me. And kicked me, and kicked me.

"You could at least fight back," Fernando said. "I mean, where's the fun in beating someone up if they aren't even gonna try to defend themselves?"

I wanted to stand, yet I didn't have the energy to do so. So, I remained on the ground. If this was my fate, then so be it. I had nothing

159

Between Love and Death

to live for now that Mom was dead. It wasn't like Archie would ever give me a second chance. Nope. There was a greater chance of pigs flying than Archie seeing through Mallory's crap.

Fernando kneeled before pulling me up. It was only a matter of seconds before he grabbed me by my collar and started punching me in the face. Over, and over, and over again.

"Enough!" someone called out.

I tilted my head, struggling to keep my eyes open. Ezra shuffled into the breakroom.

"What do you think you're doing?" Ezra asked, voice echoing through the room.

"Just trying to teach this little bitch what it's like to be a real man." Fernando's grip on my collar tightened—as if that was even possible. "I mean, if you ask me, he's getting off easy. There are things I could do to this punk ass little bitch that are much worse than this."

"This ends now!" Ezra decked Fernando, making Fernando lose his balance and collapse onto the ground.

Ezra kicked Fernando in the stomach several times before forcing him up and pinning Fernando's back against the nearest wall. Ezra punched Fernando over, and over, and over again.

I couldn't lie to myself, though. Watching Ezra beat the shit out of Fernando was better than an orgasm. If Mallory wasn't going to be punished, then Fernando needed to be punished. Fair was fair. There had to be some justice in the world.

Fernando fell onto the floor after Ezra released him.

"I don't ever wanna see you bothering Chad again!" Ezra exclaimed. "Do you understand me, asshole?"

"Yes," Fernando mumbled.

"Good." Ezra cocked his head. "Come on, Chad. Let's go back to our cell."

I nodded, then Ezra guided me out of the breakroom and back towards our cell.

160

Chris Bedell

Caring about seeming weak because Ezra had to come to my aid was pointless. I needed help, and I got it. So, I wasn't about to look a gift horse in the mouth. I challenge anyone to go through their life without accepting help at least once.

SUNDAY, NOVEMBER 10

Ezra and I stood in our cell while I chuckled. I wasn't Fernando's only victim. Word reached everyone at lunch that Fernando got into a scuffle right before breakfast. Only this time Fernando wasn't lucky. Someone reported him, and now Fernando was in solitary confinement.

Ezra rubbed the back of his head. "At least now you don't have to worry about Fernando."

"You're preaching to the choir."

"I don't even wanna think about what might've happened if I hadn't stumbled upon your altercation."

"It is what it is."

Ezra shuddered. "And I thought my father was bad."

If only I was able to get a Lotto ticket, because Ezra just confirmed my thought from the other day about how he must've had a difficult childhood. The only thing that remained to be seen was if Ezra would ever feel comfortable opening up to me. In a perfect world, Ezra would be honest and vulnerable. But I couldn't always get what I wanted. And that meant I needed to meet Ezra where he was.

Loyalty was the most important quality in a person, and I had that in spades with Ezra. I wouldn't forget Ezra sticking by my side anytime soon. It was more than could be said for Archie. Since Archie and I were no longer together, that meant I didn't need to filter my opinions about Archie. More specifically, about how Archie was the biggest flake in the world. In fact, I'd go as far as to say he was looking for any reason to bail. Mallory just happened to be the one who gave him the perfect opportunity to dump me when she tricked me into confessing how I

161

Between Love and Death

framed Mallory for Tommy's murder, despite how I knew Kelly was the person who really killed Tommy.

Ezra winked. "What are you thinking about?"

"Nothing important."

He snickered. "I'll be the judge of that."

"Trust me when I say this: not every thought I have is important."

"Whatever."

I remained silent, choosing not to respond to Ezra's comment. Having a lot of time to think meant wondering what life would've been like if Mallory never started this twisted game between us. This moment wasn't my first time playing the what-if game and it certainly wouldn't be my last. Somewhere out there existed a parallel universe where Archie and I got a real chance to date without any interference from Mallory or anyone else. It was a nice idea, anyway. I mean, no harm in dreaming. At this point, life boiled down to the few fleeting moments of comfort I could find.

TUESDAY, NOVEMBER 12

I sat at a table in back of the visitor's room across from Doreen while a silence ensued between us. Getting a visit from Archie's mother was the last thing I expected. But I wasn't going to complain about getting a reprieve from the monotony of prison life.

I hoped Doreen wasn't going to yell at me, though. Getting to interact with someone besides Ezra was nice. However, I wasn't in the mood for a lecture. I didn't have to justify my life to Doreen or anyone else.

Her lips twitched. "I must be the last person you expected to see here."

"You're right about that."

"I just had to see you, Chad."

I forced a smile. "Guess I should be flattered."

162

Chris Bedell

"What the hell happened to you?" Doreen paused for a moment. "I mean, I was really rooting for you and Archie to go the distance."

"Mallory happened," I blurted.

She scrunched her eyebrows. "Truthfully, I've never been a fan of Mallory. But it is what it is. Not like I can tell my son who he can and can't date."

"She's toxic."

Doreen played with her fingers—almost as if she needed a distraction. "I don't think I ever once witnessed you raise your voice."

"I don't know what you want me to say."

"I at least hope you have a good lawyer," Doreen said. "Everyone deserves their day in court, including you."

I raised my eyebrow. "Tell me something ... does Archie know you decided to visit me?"

"No." Doreen broke eye contact. "He'd probably have a fit if he knew I was here."

"That's gutsy of you to take the risk, then."

Her face drooped. "I was very sorry to hear about your mother. I've lost several relatives to cancer, so I certainly don't envy you."

"Thanks," I murmured.

"Do you need help paying the legal fees?"

Visiting me and having a conversation with me was one thing, but I couldn't have heard Doreen correctly. Offering to pay for my lawyer wasn't exactly loaning someone flour or sugar. For a fleeting moment, my curiosity got the best of me. I couldn't help wondering why she was being so generous.

"Well?" she demanded.

A small grin tugged at the sides of my mouth. "Your help won't be necessary—I'm being represented pro bono. But thanks. That's more than some people would offer."

She elevated her eyebrows. "Who is your lawyer? If you don't mind me asking, that is?"

163

Between Love and Death

"Sonia Drayton," I revealed. "My mother found her through a friend of a friend."

Doreen giggled. "Guess it's true what they say. It pays to know people in high places."

"That it does."

"They didn't even find Kelly's body," Doreen blurted.

"I'm well aware of that."

"If there's something you aren't telling people, now would be the time to reveal it. Nobody can help you unless you help yourself."

I bit my lip. "I've been honest with my attorney. And I swear on my mother's ashes that I didn't have anything to do with Kelly's death."

Doreen rubbed her bottom lip. "Shit. I just realized how you probably didn't get to attend your mother's funeral."

"Sonia tried petitioning the judge, but you can guess how that went."

"I believe you," Doreen said. "I mean, I know that might not mean much to you. But I have no doubt about your innocence."

"It means more than you'll ever know."

"You and Archie will find your way back to each other."

There was optimistic, and then there was delusional. I didn't quite know how I should react to Doreen mentioning the possibility of Archie and I getting a redo. Mainly because so much had transpired since that fateful first day of junior year. Short of some sort of miracle, I just didn't see how my path would cross with Archie again. And maybe, that was okay. Not everyone was meant to be in my life forever, including Archie.

Something not being destined to last forever was okay. Quality was just as important as quantity. And the important thing was to try and learn something from a situation. In Archie's case, I learned I couldn't get cocky and take things for granted. My visit with Mallory at the sanitarium last April gave Mallory the ammunition to go another few rounds with me. I was now paying the price for said moment of hubris.

"Wow," I said.

164

"Forgive me for being nosey, but I've always been a firm believer in people finding their way back to each other if they're destined to be together."

I let out a nervous laugh. "No offense, but it sounds like you've been watching too many Hallmark movies."

"Guilty as charged."

"Since you're going out of your way to be nice to me, then I'm gonna be honest with you. Reconciling with Archie is the last thing on my mind. I'm not saying that to be cruel or anything. It's just the way things are."

"Understood."

"The guard is probably gonna cut our visit short soon." I let out yet another nervous chuckle. "Trust me. I know the whole routine now."

A couple of tears rolled down her cheeks. "I'm sure you do."

"Thanks again for visiting me."

"Do you want me to chat with Archie about paying you a visit?" she asked.

I sighed, unable to make eye contact with Doreen. "I want someone to be in my life because they wanna be in my life, not because I begged them to be."

"Fair enough." She stood. "Just know I'm only a phone call away if you ever need anything."

I met her gaze, almost choking on the lump in my throat. "Thanks."

"This is gonna sound cliché or corny, but I'm gonna say it anyway." Doreen drew in a deep breath. "It's what my grandmother used to say to me during difficult circumstances."

"I'll take all the advice I can get."

"This, too, shall pass."

"From your lips to God's ears."

TUESDAY, NOVEMBER 19

My popularity increased with each passing day. I was once again seated across from someone in the visitor's room. But it wasn't Sonia, Doreen, or Mallory visiting me. No. Gemma was the one who decided to visit me.

She giggled. "No offense, but it's clear that you have had better days."

"If you've come here just to insult me, then save it. You could've chatted with Mallory if you wanted to do that."

"Save your breath. I was only making a joke."

"Well, forgive me. I've lost my sense of humor."

"Anyone with even an ounce of intelligence can see how you're being framed for Kelly's murder."

I made a pig-like snort. "What was your first clue?"

Gemma glared at me.

"It was a rhetorical question," I continued.

"Lucky for you, I'm in a position to help you." A devilish grin remained plastered on Gemma's mouth. "In fact, we can help each other."

"No offense, but I'm not following you."

"I recently inherited fifty million dollars from my great aunt in addition to becoming emancipated from my parents."

I gaped. "Wow."

"I know ... shocking, right?"

"I'm still not sure what we have in common."

"Mallory."

"In case you couldn't tell, she bested me."

"Good thing we have my money."

"I already have a lawyer. But thanks ... I appreciate it."

166

"I'm not here about paying for your lawyer," Gemma said. "Although we'll need your lawyer's help with the next part of the plan. If you agree to my terms, that is."

I gave her an icy expression. Getting a break from my mundane life was one thing, but Gemma was trying my patience. She wasn't making any sense. So, Gemma needed to get to the point sooner rather than later if she wanted me to help her.

"Out with it already!" I barked.

"We're gonna have your lawyer bring a motion to dismiss the case, and I'm gonna bribe your judge to rule in our favor."

"What makes you think she'll go for that?"

"Let's just say Judge Bell has a history of shady behavior."

"How can you possibly know that?"

"I do my homework."

I snickered. "I'm sure you do. Anyway, let me guess. You wanna spring me free so we can scheme to destroy Mallory."

"Something like that."

"Forming an alliance to destroy Mallory is tempting. I'll give you that. But Mallory isn't someone to be trifled with. Just look at where I am now."

"Two heads are better than one."

"Touché."

"I'll give you half of my inheritance," Gemma said.

"You'd part with twenty-five million dollars?" I asked, almost not believing Gemma.

"Yeah, that's how much I hate Mallory."

"I'll think about it."

"That's all I can ask."

THURSDAY, NOVEMBER 21

"I can't believe you'd consider taking Gemma's offer," Ezra said while we stood in our cell.

Between Love and Death

I gave him a warning look. "Not so loud!"

"I'm sorry. How am I supposed to react to you wanting to break the law?"

"It's not like anyone would be hurt. It's just a simple bribe."

"You say it like it's a normal thing."

"What am I supposed to do?" I asked, struggling not to raise my voice while my pulse blared in my ears. "I still have months before my case goes to trial."

"I know it's not easy, but waiting is out is the way to go. Actions have consequences. And I'd hate to see this come back and bite you in the ass."

"I'm a big boy and can look after myself. But thank you. I appreciate your concern."

Ezra snarled. "What happened to your principles?"

"They failed me," I said, a humid sensation washing over me. "So, I'm gonna focus on survival."

"What about the time we spent together? Does that mean nothing to you?"

"It's not like I'm dumping you. I promise to come back for you."

Ezra rolled his eyes. "Am I supposed to thank you?"

"Why can't you accept the world isn't black and white?"

"Because there's right and wrong. And what you're doing is clearly wrong."

I looked away from Ezra. "Guess I didn't know you as well as I thought I did."

"Guess not."

I fought back tears while my back remained turned to Ezra. Saying his reaction disappointed me would've been an understatement. Life wasn't fair—Ezra of all people should've realized that. So, Ezra shouldn't have been surprised that I'd take Gemma up on her offer. No

168

telling when another chance to save myself might arise.

WEDNESDAY, NOVEMBER 27

Gemma and I once again sat across from each other at a table in the visitor's room while I counted to ten in my head. Unfortunately for me, knowing what had to be done didn't make the situation any easier. Ezra was going to be disappointed with me once I took Gemma up on her offer. I needed to be able to live with Ezra's anger. For all I knew, Ezra could dump me once I revealed my decision to him.

"Well?" Gemma pressed.

"I'm game. Let's take down Mallory once and for all."

"Excellent."

"In the spirit of full disclosure, there's something you should know."

"And what's that?"

"Mallory isn't the one who killed Tommy—Kelly did." I held eye contact with Gemma. "Although Tommy was kinda down for the count already when Kelly finished him off."

Being truthful with Gemma was best. And not because I was conscious of how bribing a judge was wrong and was wanting to try to atone in some way for what I was about to do. Secrets were toxic. If my alliance was going to last with Gemma, then we couldn't keep things from each other. Not when there was so much at stake.

"I don't care," Gemma said, shaking her head. "Mallory is still the one who set everything in motion when she blackmailed Tommy to leave town. So, it doesn't matter if she's actually the one who finished Tommy off or not. Mallory needs to suffer, and we're gonna make that happen if it's the last thing we do."

The hairs on my back rose. The phrase "the last thing we do" didn't inspire much confidence. I just hoped Gemma's words wouldn't come back to haunt us. Bad energy was the last thing we needed to deal with. Our situation was complicated enough as it was.

169

I sucked in a breath. "I just hope Sonia will be okay with filing a motion to dismiss the case."

"She's your lawyer—it's her job to represent your best interest." She leaned closer. "Although, you probably shouldn't mention the bribe."

"How stupid do you think I am?"

"Just wanted to be sure."

MONDAY, DECEMBER 2

Ezra and I stood in silence in our cell. I just dropped the bombshell on him about how I was accepting Gemma's offer. I hoped he wouldn't be too angry with me. If what we had was real, then he needed to find a way to live with what I was doing.

His scowl intensified. "This sucks, and you know it!"

"I'm sorry you feel that way."

"Don't patronize me—I'm not a little kid."

Normally, I would've agreed with Ezra about hating the phrase "I'm sorry you feel that way." But I didn't have a choice. I wasn't going to let Ezra make me feel bad for doing what I needed to do to get out of this hellhole. Besides, Ezra wasn't the one who had his back burned with a cigarette lighter or almost beaten to death. That was me.

My lips quivered. "Please keep my secret. I mean, if you ever cared about me, then you won't snitch on me."

Being manipulative was necessary no matter how much I hated doing it. Laying it on thick was the only way to ensure Ezra wouldn't betray me. My harsh words also didn't make them any less true. If what we had was real, then Ezra wouldn't hurt me. If the situation were reversed, I would've kept his secret. Doing so was the decent thing to do. Betraying me wouldn't benefit him in the long wrong. If anything, backstabbing me would hurt Ezra's chances of being sprung from this place. Once Mallory was dealt with, I'd be free to help Ezra. He still had

Chris Bedell

several months before his case went to trial, and I didn't see anyone else lining up to help him.

FRIDAY, DECEMBER 6

Wind whipped through the air while Gemma and I stood in front of her car in the parking lot. As anticipated, Judge Bell dropped the case.

"I just can't believe it!" I exclaimed.

She patted my shoulder. "Well, believe it. You're a good person, and you deserve this."

"I'm sure Ezra would disagree with that."

"Doesn't matter. Besides, I'm sure he'll come around eventually. They always do."

I sobbed. "Thanks again for helping me. You've got no idea what this means to me. And also, thanks for the leather jacket."

Gemma nodded. "You're welcome. Anyway, why don't we get out of here and get us a little justice."

"Sounds perfect." I opened the door and got in the front passenger seat while Gemma got into the driver's seat.

Gemma cocked her head. "The gun's in the glove box. We'll need it when we stop by Mallory's."

"Understood."

Gemma started the car and barreled out of the parking lot. I was absolutely, positively free. And there wasn't a damn thing Mallory could do about it. I hoped Mallory would enjoy her last couple of hours. Gemma and I were coming for Mallory, and we were playing to win. Mallory was no match for our take-no-prisoner attitude. The only thing that remained to be seen was how much Mallory would grovel and beg for mercy.

171

AFTER

MONDAY, JUNE 8

Mallory and I sat at a table outside of Starbucks. Hard to believe I was on a date with her. But I was doing what I needed to do so I could get close to her before I gutted her like a fish. The important thing to realize was that my sham relationship with Mallory wasn't meant to last forever. No, my fauxmance would be coming to end. And sooner rather than later. I could only take being tied to Mallory for so long, after all. No explanation necessary about how she wasn't a nice person.

She giggled. "Crazy to think how it's been a whole year since I ran into you and Archie after I was released from the mental hospital."

"Are you trying to make me feel guilty for my past behavior or something? I've already apologized to you."

Mallory patted my hand, almost making my skin crawl. "No, I'm honestly not trying to make you feel guilty. I just couldn't help admiring the coincidence."

"Whatever you say."

Mallory laughed louder. "Cheer up, Chad! Just be glad I'm not asking you to relocate to the opposite side of the country in the Fall."

"You're really okay with attending the same school as Archie?"

172

Chris Bedell

She shrugged. "Sure. I'd be lying if I said the situation wasn't ideal. However, even I can't turn up my nose at a full scholarship."

"Don't know how you managed to pull that one off."

Mallory gave me a mock frown. "Are you implying that I cheated?"

"Not at all. It's just that scholarships must be competitive."

"Mine was merit based, not need based."

"That's good, I guess."

She looked me over. "You sure you're okay? Wait. Don't tell me the baristas messed up your caramel macchiato?"

I slurped my drink, trying to enjoy the sweet caramel flavors electrifying my taste buds. "The barista isn't the problem."

"Then what is? Me?"

I exhaled a deep breath. "Sorry. Just can't help thinking about my mom."

"That's understandable." She paused for a moment. And if I actually thought Mallory was a decent person, then I would've thought she was trying to choose her words carefully. But no. Some people didn't have a heart, including Mallory. The sooner I accepted that fact, the better off I'd be.

Someone snickered. Then, Mallory and I shifted our gaze at the same time. Archie stood next to us. "What do we have here?" he asked.

I stood. "Give it up, Archie! Mallory is the one I wanna be with, not you. You were merely a distraction on my journey to something better."

"Ouch," Archie said.

"Don't be too hard on yourself, Archie." Mallory sipped her latte. "It was only a matter of time before Chad and I got together."

Archie whipped his head back and forth. "I think I'm gonna be sick."

Mallory batted her eyes. "Can't you try being happy for us?"

Archie wrinkled his nose. "Not if it means Chad is throwing away his life on some loser like you. It's no secret Chad can do better than you."

173

Mallory scoffed. "Am I supposed to care what you think? Because I don't. Chad's opinion is the only one that matters to me."

"Tell me something," Archie said. "Have you and Chad had sex yet?"

"That's none of your business!" I exclaimed.

Mallory pushed a lock of her hair to the side. "Chad is right. Us consummating our relationship isn't something you need to worry about. Understand?"

Archie shifted his weight towards me. "What do you see in Mallory? You know you'll never be happy with her."

"That's not your call to make," I said, my voice booming slightly.

"I'm just trying to look out for you," Archie said.

I heaved a sigh. "Don't act like I fought for you, because I didn't. Face it. The timing just wasn't meant to be."

Archie gave me a dirty look. "How can you say that?"

Mallory rose, not even bothering to push in her chair. "Archie, honey, you might wanna leave. This conversation is going around in circles. And Chad and I have better things to do than argue with you. I mean, I'm sure any guy or girl would be thrilled to go out with you."

"That's not the point," Archie quipped. "I just don't understand how you can forgive Mallory. She's the one who framed you for Kelly's murder. I mean, if it wasn't for her, then you never would've been burned with the cigarette lighter or wouldn't have almost been beaten to death. Why isn't that registering with you?"

"Someone sounds jealous," I snapped, my gaze narrowing.

Archie stared me down. "You're right, I am jealous, because I don't like seeing someone I care about throw away their future."

"You're just embarrassing yourself," Mallory said. "I mean, don't you have any dignity?"

Archie looked Mallory over. "Can you honestly tell me that you care about Chad and won't hurt him if he accidentally steps out of line?"

Mallory frowned. "Chad is my boyfriend, not a horse. Any issues that come up will be dealt with respect and care. Because that's what people do when they're in a relationship. Or have you forgotten that part?"

Archie folded his arms. "You're the one who arranged for me to overhear Chad's confession last summer. I mean, you seemed pretty happy to mess with Chad's life then."

"I'll admit it," Mallory said. "I'm selfish, and want Chad all to myself. Especially when I'm so much better for him than you."

"If you believe that, then you're more delusional than I ever thought," Archie said.

"Just leave!" Mallory pleaded.

Archie gave me a somber look. "Starbucks was our special place."

"I have new traditions now," I said.

Archie snickered. "Forget about sex. I bet you two don't even kiss."

"We kiss plenty." Mallory leaned forward before I could process what was about to happen, and she kissed me.

A twinge of nausea overcame me while Mallory and I kissed. Living in a house without air conditioning was preferrable to making out with Mallory. But I didn't have a choice in the matter. I needed to do what needed to be done to sell my relationship with Mallory. No point in imploding things when I was so close to getting what I wanted.

Mallory pulled back from me, then shot daggers at Archie. "Satisfied?"

"Hardly. Anyway, call me when you dump Mallory." Archie smacked his shoulder against mine, then darted down the street while a light breeze trickled through the air. Archie was soon out of sight.

My Adam's apple throbbed. "I'm sorry about that. Running into Archie was the last thing I expected to happen tonight."

"Don't worry about it—not like you planned for us to intentionally run into your ex-boyfriend."

Between Love and Death

"Hopefully you aren't gonna let what Archie said get to you. He's just upset because he's unable to hump everything that moves."

"That's one way of putting it," Mallory said, smiling.

"I know our relationship isn't perfect, but it can be pretty damn close if we decide to put in the work."

"Agreed.

MONDAY, JUNE 15

Archie and I lay on our backs in my bedroom with the bed comforter wrapped around both of us. Mallory bailed on grabbing dinner because of a migraine. So, I decided to take advantage of the moment and spend some time with my boyfriend.

"I hate having to sneak around," Archie said.

"It won't be forever."

"It better not be."

"It won't." My throat tightened. "I'm putting an end to everything tomorrow night. The situation has gone on long enough."

Archie moved his body so he was now looking me in the eye. "What's the plan exactly?"

"I'll let you know once the details are finalized."

"I don't mean to be a downer, but you can't leave anything to chance. Not when dealing with someone like Mallory."

No doubt existed in my mind that Archie meant well. However, he should've known better than to make that kind of comment. I of all people knew not to underestimate Mallory. I wouldn't forget how I landed in prison because of her.

"I'm just glad she seems to have bought your outburst." My breathing slowed down, returning to normal. "Mallory catching onto us is the last thing we need."

Archie pouted. "We didn't even get to attend prom together or go to a graduation party."

Chris Bedell

"We'll have other things to celebrate. Don't tell me you have buyer's remorse?" I asked. "No offense, but you're the one who joined Gemma and I after you almost died."

"I'm aware of that. Guess I'm just more impatient than I realized."

"Maybe we can take a cruise when this thing is over. If you want to, that is."

He gave me a small smile. "That'd be nice."

Thank goodness Archie didn't fight me about taking a vacation once Mallory was dealt with. If he had, then I didn't know what I would've done. Between Archie's family money and Gemma giving me half of her inheritance, money wasn't an issue. That meant Archie and I would have to take a fancy vacation. Something that bordered on sinful decadence. It was what we deserved after everything that transpired during the last two years of school. I mean, we couldn't change the past. But we could try forget it. Nice idea, anyway.

I let out another deep breath. "It's not like I'm enjoying my time with Mallory. Hopefully, you know that."

"Yes, I understand how cozying up to Mallory is just a means to an end."

"Good. I'd hate for you to get the wrong idea."

Archie let out a small laugh. "Guess I can't blame Mallory for being obsessed with you. I mean, you're pretty amazing."

"Thanks."

"I'm serious, Chad."

"I'd like to think my mother and Ezra are friends in heaven."

He nudged me. "Way to change the subject."

"I'm sorry … did you wanna continue talking about Mallory?"

"No, we can discuss your mother and Ezra if you want to."

I rubbed my hand up and down my head. "Ezra being against Gemma bribing the judge should've been the clue that my relationship with him wasn't meant to last. I mean, I'm sorry that he's dead.

177

However, he had no right to judge me. It's a cruel world and sometimes you gotta make the tough choice."

"Spoken like a real politician."

My shoulders shook. "Shoot me if I ever decide to run for office."

"Seriously?"

"No, I was making a joke."

"Oh, okay. Good." Archie stretched. "You've definitely experienced enough violence to last several lifetimes."

"No shit."

"Anyway, going back to your mother and Ezra … you believe in Heaven?"

"It'd be nice to think people find peace once they finish their lives on earth. What about you?"

Archie shrugged. "Truthfully, I've never given the issue much thought."

"Understandable. I mean, I don't mean to state the obvious, but you have your whole life ahead of you."

"Damn straight."

"It's okay if you're nervous about the Mallory thing," I said. Archie looped his arms around me, looking me right in the eye. "It'd only mean you're human."

"I know. I know."

TUESDAY, JUNE 16

Mallory and I sat on my living room couch, enjoying wine and cheese and crackers. More specifically, Moscato wine. I felt like something sweet, and Mallory hadn't argued with me. There was no reason for her to bicker with me about the wine selection. Free booze was free booze.

I grabbed a cracker, then sipped my wine. I let the wine's sweet flavor linger in my mouth before swallowing it.

Mallory beamed. "You were right to go with the Moscato."

178

"Thanks, I appreciate that."

"I would've taken you for a dry wine like Chardonnay. But no big deal."

"I'm glad you see it my way."

She grinned. "Relationships are about compromise."

Fuck it. I couldn't listen to one more minute of Mallory rambling. I checked the pillow case behind me. There was one problem–the gun wasn't there.

Mallory cackled, and I lifted my gaze off the couch. She flashed the gun at me. "Looking for this?" she asked.

"Huh?"

"I found it when you were in the bathroom."

Shit. Guess I had myself to blame for Mallory stealing the gun. I should've known better than to leave a firearm unattended to. Especially when dealing with someone as unstable as Mallory. No telling what might prompt Mallory to shoot me or anyone else. Crazy was crazy. There was no reasoning with some people. And it didn't make me harsh to believe that idea. I was just being practical.

Her eyes lit up while she continued holding the gun. "How stupid do you think I am, Chad? I know the last couple of months was a ploy to get close to me."

"Then why did you do go along with it?"

She pointed the gun at me, fingers on the trigger. "I could say that I was curious about how far you would go. But that'd be a lie. I was playing you as much as you were playing me. And I should thank you for providing the weapon."

I squinted. "Wait. You were planning on killing me tonight?"

"Yeah, I was."

"Why?"

"This toxic feud between us isn't gonna end until one of is dead. Surely, you must be aware of that?"

"I didn't want it to be this way, but you didn't give me a choice."

Between Love and Death

"You had your life back once Gemma got you out of jail!" Mallory shouted. "But no. You kept antagonizing me."

I let out a nervous laugh. "Guess I shouldn't be surprised about you once again deciding to play the victim."

"I'll give you points for trying, though. You lasted longer than I thought you would." A vein on Mallory's head surfaced. "But you didn't actually think I'd believe that little ruse you and Archie created, did you?"

"You knew about that, too?"

"It was kinda obvious."

"Yet you went along with it."

"Guess I'm better at biding my time than you," Mallory said.

Sweat tumbled down my back. Mallory still had the gun pointed at me, and I didn't know how much longer I could keep the conversation going. I didn't need a crystal ball to realize Mallory would get tired of talking.

"If you're gonna kill me, then I at least deserve an answer about Kelly," I said.

She cackled. "What do you want to know?"

"Is Kelly alive?"

"Yes, she is."

"How did you get her to go along with this?"

"It's really quite an interesting story. However, we don't have time for that."

"Come on, Mallory. Does it matter if you kill me now or five minutes from now?"

She winked. "I've got things to do."

"Like what?"

"Like living my life. And it's a shame you can't be part of it. But it is what it is at this point. Because, yes, I do wish things had been different between us. You just rejected me the first day of junior year without any consideration of my feelings. How could you be so cruel?"

180

Chris Bedell

Mallory might as well have just shot me right here in the living room if she was going to drone on about me rejecting her. People couldn't always get what they wanted out of life, and Mallory would do best to understand that.

Mallory took in a deep breath. "If it makes you feel better, Kelly wasn't a willing participant. I had to blackmail her."

"With what?"

"I threatened to kill her boyfriend if she didn't help me."

"Didn't even know she was seeing anyone at the time."

"Me neither. At least not at first." Mallory coughed into her left arm while her right hand remained on the gun that was aimed at me. "Any last words, Chadwick?"

If Mallory hadn't lost her mind before, she had now. Nobody had ever referred to me as Chadwick. It wasn't lost on me that Mallory must've called me "Chadwick" as a way to dehumanize me.

"Go to Hell!" I touted.

"You first."

Gunshots echoed. But I wasn't the one who was shot. Someone fired two shots at Mallory and she collapsed onto the couch, stomach side down. Blood oozed out of Mallory's back while my breathing became more labored. Another gunshot reverberated through the air, once again piercing Mallory in the back.

I stood, then turned my head. Kelly was about fifteen feet away from me.

"What the hell?" I stammered.

Kelly cracked a small smile. "I believe the phrase you're looking for is 'you're welcome.'"

"But how?" I asked.

"Mallory and I inherited a house from a cousin a couple of years ago." Kelly shoved the gun into her inside jacket pocket. "It's where Mallory has been making me stay."

Between Love and Death

"It can't be a coincidence that you broke into my house at the exact moment Mallory was gonna kill me."

"You're right, it isn't." Kelly paused for a moment. "Mallory told me she intended to kill you this evening."

"Where'd you even get the gun?"

"You don't wanna know."

"So what? She gave you free reign of the cabin?"

"More or less."

"What are we gonna do?" I asked. "It's not like we can wrap this up in a neat bow."

"No offense, but this isn't my problem," Kelly said, not even flinching. "I saved your life because that was the decent thing to do. But you're on your own with this one."

Shock bubbled inside. "You're not gonna help me?"

"Afraid not."

"Let me guess. You and your boyfriend are gonna leave the country with fake passports or something?"

"Something like that."

My eyebrows knitted together. "How'd you even make plans to leave the country on such short notice? I can't imagine Mallory would be happy if she discovered you were chatting with your former boyfriend."

"She gave me a burner phone for emergencies," Kelly replied. "But what she didn't know was that I had it with pretending to be dead. So, I decided to take fate into my own hands."

"I would say it was nice seeing you, but we both know that wouldn't be true."

"Yeah, save your energy. You've got more important things to do

182

than making small-talk with me."

"I can't believe Mallory was onto you," Archie said sometime later while he, Gemma, Rebecca, Dan, and I stood in the woods in back of my house digging a hole.

I grunted. "Guess I'm not as clever as I thought I was."

Gemma stopped digging for a moment. "I knew Archie and I should've been there for backup."

"Now I feel like a fool for ever thinking Mallory was a good person," Rebecca said.

Dan glanced at Rebecca. "Don't beat yourself up. She had everyone fooled."

"I'd just like to know we're gonna get away with this," Rebecca said.

Gemma's hair bobbed in the wind. "I'll hack into Mallory's Facebook and post that she changed her mind about going to college in the Fall and is opting to travel instead."

"That's great," Rebecca spat, face turning bright red. "But that still leaves the problem of contacting the college on Mallory's behalf."

"I'll take care of that, too," Gemma said.

I stared at Rebecca and Dan. "Thank you for helping Archie, Gemma, and I. It isn't lost on me how you didn't have to do this."

Rebecca continued digging, sending dirt flying. "As long as this means we're friends again, then I'm happy to help."

"Fair enough," I said.

Leaving the past in the past was best. I had been friends with Rebecca and Dan once before and I could be friends with them again. Holding onto anger wouldn't get me anywhere. Mallory was proof of that, after all. Mallory's anger cost Mallory her life.

Archie's jaw quaked. "Just hope nobody saw us taking the tarp to the woods."

183

"The body was covered," Gemma said. "Besides, people move tarps all the time. You know how people are about doing their yard work."

THUESDAY, JUNE 25

Waves crashed onto the sand while a salty aroma wafted through the air as Archie and I sat on our towels at one of the local beaches. In fact, I'd even go as far as to say the universe was on our side for once. Archie and I had the entire beach to ourselves, and I wouldn't have it any other way. Archie and I deserved a picturesque moment after everything we had been through because of Mallory.

I bit down hard. "I wasn't honest with you, Arch."

"No shit. It didn't take a genius to realize you must've omitted some details of what happened."

"Mallory was going to kill me, that part is true. But I didn't get back possession of the gun." I picked at one of my nails. "Kelly is alive. She's the one who shot Mallory, not me."

"And she left you to deal with everything?"

"Yup."

"Do you have any idea about where she is now?" he asked.

"Something about leaving the country."

"That sounds like a good idea."

I blinked. "Really?"

"You and I did discuss the possibility of a vacation once the Mallory situation was dealt with once and for all."

"How about Tahiti?" I asked.

"I'm game."

A few seagulls landed onto the beach several feet away from Archie and I and started foraging for food. For the first time in a long time, I'd be able to get a goodnight's sleep. Mallory was absolutely, positively dead. The situation might not have gone down exactly like I wanted it to, but it didn't matter. The monster had been slayed.

Chris Bedell

So, yeah. My life was going to be okay. I just knew it.

185

Chris Bedell has published over a dozen novels. He also graduated with a BA in Creative Writing from Fairleigh Dickinson University in 2016.

www.ingramcontent.com/pod-product-compliance
Lightning Source LLC
LaVergne TN
LVHW031204040125
800523LV00004B/418